THEIR KINGDOM COME

A DARK BULLY ROMANCE (THE SINNERS OF SAINT AMOS BOOK 1)

LOGAN FOX

WARNING

This dark romance is a work of fiction. The aim of this book is to entertain, not educate. While it includes elements of BDSM, it in no way depicts a healthy relationship (kinky or otherwise). That being said, you can expect some pretty dark content such as non-con, dub-con, public humiliation and degradation, violence, knife play, breath play, choking, murder, mention of suicide and abuse. Please tread carefully if you have triggers.

JOIN THE FOX DEN

Can I send you my secret dark romance novella that's never been published…?
Join my VIP newsletter and you'll receive your own exclusive copy of My Darling, and I'll keep you up to date with my new releases and promos!
https://authorloganfox.com/my-darling-signup

PLAYLIST

Theme Song

The In-Between — In This Moment

Playlist

Pet — A Perfect Circle
Never Enough — Fetish
Imagine — A Perfect Circle
Crawling — Dream State
The Trauma Model — King 810
Call Me Devil — Friends in Tokyo
Touched Your Skin — Landon Tewers
Soldier — Fleurie
How Deep Is Your Love — The Bros. Landreth

To view this playlist, please visit my website at https://
authorloganfox.com/playlists.

PROLOGUE

Exodus, Matthews, and Ephesians say you must honor your father and your mother. Guess it's only fair then—the day my parents and me have the worst fight in history is the last day I see them.

And what was the fight about?

Clothes.

New clothes. Since I'd literally worn holes in all of mine.

Mom promised we'd go buy some as soon as Dad came home. There was a sale on at the mall, so the timing was perfect. I knew exactly what I wanted too — we'd be back way before the night service at our church.

But Dad ran late, and because Dad didn't believe in things like cellphones, we had to wait for him. I mean, he knew they existed, obviously, but he saw them as materialistic trappings.

Clothes fell under that category too.

When he finally arrived, there wasn't enough time for us to go.

I guess the planets aligned or some shit because for the first time in my life, at the age of seventeen, I threw a tantrum.

I yelled. I screamed. I swore.

They said nothing. And then they left and went to church without me.

It's weird to think that if we hadn't had that fight, things would have been so much different.

For instance, I'd be dead.

But I hadn't been in the car when they'd hit the black ice on the road. I'd been in my robe and slippers, sulking into a cup of hot chocolate.

I never finished that chocolate.

I don't even know what happened to it.

Someone must have taken it to the kitchen, tossed it out, cleaned it.

But it wasn't me.

Because I was at a police station for most of the rest of the night, pretending to understand what they kept telling me.

My parents were dead.

Just like I should have been dead.

Something did die that night, something deep inside. Back then, I'd thought it was a precious, sacred thing like love.

Turns out I was wrong.

The only thing that perished that night were the invisible chains keeping me tethered to a life I silently hated with every breath.

I didn't die that night.

I was set free.

And it changed everything.

"For those who believe, no proof is necessary. For those who don't believe, no proof is possible."

STUART CHASE

1
TRINITY

There's a loud thump. My head bounces off the window of the cab, and my eyes fly open in surprise. I squint out at the blurring landscape as my mind scrambles to figure out where the hell I am while my heart tries to climb out of my throat.

"Sorry 'bout that. Road's not exactly in the best condition."

I glance over at the cab driver, and swipe the back of my hand over my mouth. Had I been drooling in my sleep? I'd been out cold—dreaming again. A happy dream this time. One where my parents were still alive.

"How long till we get there?" I mumble, trying to work out the kink in my neck. Outside, colossal birch and maple trees block out everything but a strip of gray sky. There's another thump, followed by a rattle, as the cab's wheels skate over another pothole.

"A few more minutes."

Hugging myself, I turn and stare out my window. Better than watching the cab driver's eyes in the rear-view mirror. We've spent over two hours together, and barely said a word.

We passed through the last town at least an hour ago and

we've been heading deeper into West Virginia ever since. At least I know where I'm going. For the first time since that policeman knocked on our front door, there's some kind of order to my life.

"There it is," the driver says as we round a corner.

He didn't have to—my eyes latched onto the all-boys boarding school the second it appeared through the windshield.

Holy crap.

My mouth goes dry. "That's Saint Amos?"

I feel his eyes on me, and we make eye contact in the mirror. "Isn't it a little late in the year to be starting boarding school?"

Heat touches my cheeks. "I…don't have a choice."

The last hundred yards or so, the dilapidated tar road smooths into a hard-packed dirt road. The closer we get and the more the building looms, the deeper my stomach sinks.

This place looks more like Dracula's castle than a boarding school. There aren't statues of demons and things on the facade, but with its multitude of spires and fancy moldings, it's undeniably Gothic. Before Dracula could live here, someone would have to remove the enormous crucifix above the front entrance.

The trees thin. An immaculately trimmed lawn spreads like a pool of green algae around the base of the massive, sprawling structure.

The driver maneuvers the cab around a fountain where a concrete, pigeon-shit stained Virgin Mary is nursing baby Jesus.

Some of those streaks look like tears.

"Need help with your things?" the driver asks.

I huff as I shake my head. "I can manage, thanks."

He nods as he brakes and puts the car into park. "Good luck, and God bless."

My mouth tightens, but I give him another nod and drag my duffel bag out with me. That and my backpack are the only things I have with me. Our family wasn't big on material possessions like clothes, or jewelry, or furniture. In fact, the only thing they were big on was *that*.

I tip my head back and stare up at the crucifix.

I hope it stays up there. It could crush someone if it were to fall.

There's a rattle of gravel as the cab driver pulls away, and I turn to watch him until the shadow of the distant maples dapples the roof of his car.

The best way out is through, right?

I wince as I bang the big brass knocker on the door. Every person inside must have heard that racket.

But nothing happens.

I shuffle my feet and glance around as I wait, then try again.

The door shifts inward.

Guess there's no point in locking things around here. Who the hell's going to rob this place? It's miles away from anything.

I push open the door and step into cool, damp shadows that cling to me like a film. I'm in a vast entrance hall. Small, stained glass windows barely let enough light through to illuminate the double staircase. On a brighter day this place would look magnificent. Right now it's like I'm starring in my own horror movie.

"Hello?" My voice hurriedly warbles back to me as if it's terrified to venture deeper inside.

Lord, it's quiet in here.

Where is everyone?

Surely *someone* had to know I was coming.

"Are you Trinity?"

My heart leaps into my throat, strangling a gasp. I whirl around.

A kid a few years younger than me stands in the shadows beside the doorway. Dressed in brown slacks, a dress shirt with a brown tie, and a brown blazer, he looks like the adolescent version of Mr. Bean, especially with his dark, slicked-down hair. He squints at me like he's trying to figure out if I'm real or a ghost.

Where the hell did he come from?

"That's me." I try and sound jolly but I probably look more like a lunatic. "And you are?"

"Jasper. I'm your roommate." Judging from the faint scowl on his face, he's not thrilled with the fact. He strolls past me, heading for the left set of stairs winding up to a landing.

I tighten my grip on my duffel bag and readjust the strap of my backpack before following. Our footsteps echo hollowly until we reach the wooden stairs. "Roommate?" I call out after him. "So we don't get our own rooms?"

"Duh," he says dryly.

Holy crap, I'm just trying to make conversation. I didn't ask to be here any more than he did. And I know he's not here by choice, because no one would be here by choice. This is the place bad souls go to await sentencing.

Damp. Dark. *Dismal.*

Jasper turns into a hallway leading off the landing. Almost immediately, he takes another turn. Then another. A minute later, I stop trying to keep track of where we're headed.

Flickering sodium lights cast an ugly yellow glare over the doorways and somber portraits we pass.

Holy crap, it's cold. Two weeks until summer break, and it could be the middle of winter.

I'm wearing a black cardigan, a vest, and jeans with the hems turned up so I don't step on them. The thin wool covering my arms could have been tissue paper for all the protection it's offering me. I'm tempted to let down my mass of black curls, if only for some extra warmth around my neck.

What I know about Saint Amos could barely fill a serviette. It's an all-boys, faith-orientated prep school specializing in training new priests. But I didn't come here for their theological program—I'm here because it's the only place where even a remnant of my previous life still exists.

His name is Father Gabriel. Technically, he's all the family I have left. If it weren't for him, I'd still be a ward of the state. Enrolling at Saint Amos wasn't my first choice, but I'm starting to realize orphans don't get a say in how their lives are run.

Luckily I'm used to having all my major life decisions made for me.

"So how long have you been here?"

"Too long," Jasper replies stiffly.

What did I do to piss him off? Is this because he has to share a room with me? I glance at the multitude of doorways we've passed in this stretch of hallway alone. It's impossible that every room in this place is occupied. So why do I have to share with a boy?

I should make an effort to be friends, especially if I'm going to be living with this kid. "I'm sorry if I kept you waiting," I say.

He lets out a sigh and gives a half-hearted shrug without looking back at me.

On this level, we pass several stained glass windows, none of which look as if they can be opened. Most are random arrangements of colored glass, but the larger ones form crude images.

Doves flying toward rays of heavenly light.

Various saints and angels.

People tilling the soil under a watchful eye. Literally, an eye in the sky—lead strips for lashes and everything.

"Place used to be a Catholic orphanage," the kid says.

"It's..." I want to say beautiful, but that would be an outright lie. "Impressive."

We take another set of stairs, putting us on the fourth floor. Wooden doors crowd the walls of the passage. Small cards slipped behind tiny brass frames centered below each doorway's arch bear the room's number.

Jasper leads me to room 113.

He opens it and steps inside.

"You don't lock doors around here?"

He turns and gives me a dead-eyed stare. "You got something to hide?"

I laugh as I enter the room, but I cut it off a second later.

It looks more like a prison cell than a bedroom. Even the small window is meshed with a steel frame as if to stop anyone from climbing out and jumping. Two cots—one against each wall—fill most of the space. What's left is crowded out by a double-door closet and a desk with a set of drawers on each side of the gap where the chair fits in.

Jasper points at one of the beds. "That's mine."

"You sure?" I mumble to myself. The beds look identical. In fact, I wouldn't have been surprised if he'd told me no one lived in this room.

"That's yours," he says, pointing at the left-hand closet door. "Stay out of my side."

"Why, you got something to hide?"

He turns angry eyes on me, and I bite down on my lip.

It's been a long day. Hell, it's been a long month.

My duffel bag and backpack thump to the floor. This place reeks of mothballs and stale air but if I can open the window that might help.

The window is sealed shut.

Jasper grabs something out of his drawer. "I got class," he says before walking out.

I rush over to the door and poke my head out in the hall. "Hey!"

My voice booms back at me. Jasper swings around, but he doesn't stop walking.

"Where do I go?"

Jasper shrugs. "Only told me to show you the room!" he yells back before disappearing around the corner.

"Mother of God," I mutter to myself as I step back into the room. I stare out the doorway, and shiver when a damp breeze slips inside. "Surprised no one gets pneumonia." I push the door closed and let out another sigh as I sink onto the corner of my bed.

It groans theatrically under my weight, and I roll my eyes.

This is what happens when the only thing going through your head for days at a time is the mantra, *what else could possibly go wrong?*

I challenged the Universe, and it came at me swinging.

2
TRINITY

I'm glad everything I own fits into two bags. There's barely enough space on my side of the closet to hang the few dresses and jeans I have. Even the four cubbyholes on my side of the cabinet are barely large enough to fit a pair of shoes.

I take my fat, leather-bound bible and perch reluctantly on the creaky bed with it my lap. I trace my fingers over the gold title embossed on the cover. Then I flip it open and take out the photo nestled between the first few pages.

My father's stern eyes stare out at me from a decade past. He looks dashing in his full clerical vestments, despite his no-nonsense expression. I wish I had a photo of mom too—even better, the three of us together—but my parents considered photos a form of vanity, much like having more than three sets of clothes to rotate out during any given week.

Or makeup.

Or jewelry.

If they knew they would die months before my eighteen birthday, would things have been different? Would we have spent less time in church and more time in the park, or going to the beach, or playing ball in the backyard?

Nope.

I open the first drawer and put the bible inside, shoving it as far back as I can.

I have no intention of reading it. I only brought it along because Mother treasured it so. I didn't even know about the photo until I accidentally dropped the book on its spine while I was collecting my things from home a week ago.

Twenty-seven days.

Not even a month since they've been gone, and it already feels like a lifetime ago. I only remember bits and pieces since then, and most of those I try to forget.

Fuck you.

I kick the drawer closed with my ballerina pump.

"First day and you're already destroying school property?"

I'm on my feet in a second and whirl around to face the door. There's a guy in the doorway, leaning with his shoulder against the jamb.

He's tall and lean-muscled with a sharp nose, angular jaw, and hooded blue eyes. I wouldn't be in the least surprised if he turned out to be a fashion model despite his military-style haircut that leaves little more than a layer of fuzz on his perfectly shaped head. We didn't have magazines around the house, but I saw them once or twice in the library. He's wearing Saint Amos's school uniform, but his collar is loose, and his tie crooked.

A smug smile carves a dimple into his cheek. "You miss the turn off for Sisters of Mercy or something?" He runs his gaze down my body before snapping them back to my eyes. "Or did you somehow miss the fact that this in all-boys school when you enrolled?"

What the hell is he talking about? I shake my head, and stagger back when he slips inside the room.

"Can you talk?" He glances about the room as if the answer doesn't concern him. "Or are you an orphan and a mute?"

I'm starting to wonder the same thing, because I seem incapable of forming words. It doesn't help that he keeps moving closer, and the only way to keep my distance in this tiny room would be to climb over the bed.

"'Cos I'm pretty sure they'd tell the hallway monitor to expect a mute orphan." His eyes flicker to me. "Especially one as adorably fuckable as you."

Hallway monitor? My cheeks flare with heat. "Excuse me?" I bark out before I can stop myself.

"Aw," the guy says, pouting lush lips. "You just became slightly less tragic."

"Who the hell are you?"

Air whistles through his teeth. He rushes forward. The closet door bangs as he pushes me up against it so hard, the air knocks out of my lungs.

"Blasphemous little slut," he hisses. I open my mouth to scream.

His fingers wrap around my throat, and suddenly yelling for help isn't an option anymore. He leans close enough for his breath to caress my lips. "I don't like surprises." His voice is dangerously low.

"Please," I manage, grabbing his wrists and digging my fingernails into his skin.

He doesn't even seem to notice. "Maybe you're not even a girl," he whispers, his mouth so close to my ear that his lips brush my skin. "Is that why they sent you here?" His free hand skims across my stomach and latches onto the top of my jeans. With a twist of his wrist, the button pops open.

"Only one way to find out, isn't there?" he murmurs. His fingertips slide behind the elastic band of my underwear.

My body goes stiff. Nothing exists but his creeping fingers.

A gong sounds out.

It's not exceptionally loud, but it's so unexpected I jerk in surprise. His fingertips slip out from behind my underwear.

He steps back. Cool air rushes down my throat. I cough, sagging against the closet as he studies me.

"Saved by the bell," he says through a laugh. His face transforms into a hard, unfriendly mask. "See you around, slut."

Then he's gone.

I count ten thundering heartbeats before I dare go over to the door and check if he truly has left. The hallway outside is empty. Slamming closed the door, I back up into the room until the bed knocks into the back of my knees. I sit on automatic, staring at the door through wide eyes.

How the hell am I supposed to process what just happened?

Who was that guy?

Why on earth did he—

I flinch at a knock on the door. Swallow.

He's back.

But of course it's not him. He's not the kind of guy to knock.

So what fresh hell is this then?

"Trinity?"

Another knock.

I jump to my feet and race to throw open the door.

A man in his late thirties regards me from across the threshold. His mouth is set in a gentle curve.

"Good to see you again, Trinity," he says, his warm chestnut brown eyes wrinkling in the corners as his smile inches up.

"Father Gabriel! It's—"

A wave crashes down on me, choking the words. His is the first familiar face I've seen in weeks.

I'd never known what loneliness was. The longest I'd been apart from my parents had been a few hours. But from that moment the bell rang, and I opened the door, and I saw a police officer standing where I'd been expecting my parents—perhaps Mom juggling a bag of groceries while she hunted for her keys, or Dad looking sheepish because he'd left his pair inside the house—I'd had no one.

No one.

A week later I realized the policeman hadn't come to tell me my parents had died in a car accident. He'd come to say nothing would ever be the same again. I was destined for a dark, lonely future where flowers didn't bloom, the sun no longer shone, and food had lost its taste.

For weeks, I've been handed from person to person like a goddamn parcel with no return address, the receiver simply marked as 'To Whom it May Concern'.

Strong arms wrap around me, squeeze me, warm me. Cigarette smoke and candle wax waft up to me in a familiar and oh so comforting smell.

A sob wracks me. I cling to Father Gabriel like I'd fall if I were to let go.

My knees weaken when he strokes my head and murmurs, "Hush, child. You're safe now."

3
TRINITY

Pulling away from Father Gabriel is one of the most difficult things I've had to do in weeks, and that includes identifying my parents at the morgue. But I'm behaving like a kid, and he's the last person I want to disappoint. So I suck up my sorrow, and wriggle out of his arms. My smile isn't as steady as I want it to be, but at least it's there.

I know I should tell him about the guy who was just here. What he'd been about to do. But the thought of relaying those sordid details makes my stomach shrivel up with humiliation. What'll it change, anyway? It might make him even angrier.

"Are you all settled?" Gabriel asks, using a knuckle to swipe a tear from my cheek.

"Yeah."

"Then I'll show you around." He holds out an arm, his smile inching up when I take it.

He looks odd in his pale, cable-knit sweater and dark slacks. His loafers barely make a sound as he leads me out of the room. I guess he only wears his official clerical garb when he's visiting a member of his congregation.

I pause, and then lean back to pull the door closed. He pats my arm, his smile growing a little sad around the edges.

"You're safe now, child. This is the Lord's house. He will watch over you while you're under His roof."

I think back to the stained glass window, the one with that big eye in the sky with the people toiling beneath it. And then the guy who slipped into my room.

If God was watching me, then it seems He was more interested in seeing how far he'd get than putting a stop to it.

But then a bell rang, and he stopped. I'd call that divine intervention, wouldn't you?

"Thank you," I murmur, dropping my gaze. My cheeks grow hot again. "I don't know what I would have done if you hadn't become my guardian."

"A foster home is no place for a child of God," he says. "Especially one as bright and talented as you. I'm more than happy to help."

I manage a smile. Seeing Gabriel has brought back too many memories. They fill my mind as he leads me down the hall, and my mood dips ever lower.

Father Gabriel had been the bishop of our parish for close to five years before he left the country for missionary work a few months ago. My father, the priest of our local congregation, had known him since the start of his seminary training, where Father Gabriel had been one of his tutors.

Gabriel was at our house at least three times a week, and often ate dinner with us. He was my parents' closest friend, and from what I could gather, their confidant when their marriage became a little rocky. That was way back before I was even born.

"I must apologize for not meeting you when you arrived. This close to summer, I have a hundred and one tasks." Gabriel laughs. "I'm sure the staff is looking forward to this break as much as the students."

I laugh with him and it sounds strange out here in the dimly lit hallways. "This place is enormous. How many students are here?"

"Just shy of five hundred."

My mouth sets. I shouldn't be ungrateful, but it begs the question. Before I can bring myself to ask it, though, Gabriel says, "You're wondering why you don't have your own room." His mouth forms that all too familiar neutral line. "As much as I'd like to give you one, doing so would set a bad precedent. Students at Saint Amos must earn their privileges."

"And a private room is a privilege," I say, nodding along. I guess it would be unfair for me to be elevated above students who've been here for years already. And the last thing I want to do is stand out.

"So…does that mean Jasper lost his privileges?"

"God rewards our faith in many ways, Trinity. But he also demands penance for our sins."

"What did Jasper do?" I ask, voice hushed. I'm guessing a private room is one of the best privileges around here. I could be wrong, but it would make sense why Jasper is acting so damn sulky.

"That's between him and God."

Gabriel pauses by a window. It's the first one with clear glass I've noticed, and the first with a latch. I glance down both sides of the hall. I have no idea where I am. How long is it going to take me to figure out this place?

He pushes open the window and breathes in the air rushing in from outside, then beckons me over with a flip of his hand.

I go to stand beside him. My breath catches.

"Oh my Lo—" I cut off, biting down on my lip just in time. *Blasphemous little slut.*

"If you think it's beautiful now, wait till the leaves turn." There's a reverential hush to his voice.

"I can't wait."

Even though we're on the third level of this majestic building, trees soar up and around us. It's as if the school was dropped into the middle of the forest and left to its own defenses.

"Can you see where the grounds end?" Gabriel points, and I follow his finger.

"Yeah?"

"Anything past that fence is out of bounds," he says firmly. "Understand?"

I look at him and nod. "I understand."

"It may look innocent, but the forest is a dangerous place," he adds, his brown eyes searching mine. "We've lost more students than I care to admit out there. I wouldn't want that to happen to you, child."

Lost them?

My neck moves like a rusty joint when I turn to look out the window again.

The forest doesn't look like a place I'd want to go anyway. Why on earth would anyone have to be warned to stay away?

"Come on. Lots to see before lunch."

This time, Father Gabriel doesn't hold out his arm. I wish he had—the dark and the cold of this place is pressing in again. I suppress a shiver as I follow him down the hall, and glance back at the window. From this angle, only a sliver of gray sky is visible.

What happened to those kids? Did they lose their way and starve?

Or did something else find them first?

"I 'm sorry I wasn't there for you when your parents passed," Father Gabriel says out of nowhere. We've been walking for about ten minutes, and passed another two windows—both with dramatically different views than the first.

Saint Amos is more like a small town than a school. This building contains the staff quarters, the student's rooms, the administration office, the kitchens, the washrooms, and the dining hall.

Outside, there's a chapel, a building that houses the classrooms, and even a crypt. From the window we viewed it at, the rectangular shapes of concrete slabs placed on the handful of graves beside the crucifix shaped building were visible.

Yet another place I have absolutely no interest in visiting, although Father Gabriel hadn't warned me to stay away this time.

Further back on the property are the stables and some sports grounds—even a gymnasium with an indoor pool.

"Trinity?"

I snap out of my thoughts. "The social worker said you were away on missionary work?"

He smiles at this. "South America. It's so rewarding to share God's message to impoverished nations."

Father Gabriel did a lot of missionary work. My father's even been overseas with him more than once. They would stay away for up to months at a time. Dad always seemed different when he came back, but I could never figure out why.

I guess spreading the gospel changes you.

"Judging from your grades, your parents did an excellent job homeschooling you." Gabriel chuckles. "Our classes are slightly larger, but trust me, your academics won't suffer. We have excellent teachers. Some of them past students, in fact."

Dad taught me scripture. *Mom* taught me everything else. But I don't say anything—I've never been one to pick a fight.

We descend a stairwell and arrive in a vast hallway. Several yards away, it ends in a set of double doors. Through the small windows set in them, I can make out a bustle of activity beyond.

The dining hall? My stomach grumbles. When was the last time I ate something? It might have been yesterday, but I can't remember if it was breakfast or lunch. They'd served supper on the train last night, but I'd been too nervous to eat anything.

I start forward, expecting Father Gabriel to move ahead. I come up short when he grasps my elbow and gently turns me around to face him.

My chest grows tight at the look on his face. "What?" I ask quietly.

He releases me and grasps his hands in front of him.

I know Father Gabriel well. He looks older today. He's still far from an old man, but his face has lost some of its youthful glow.

"Anyone can lose their faith, Trinity." Tiny creases form at the corners of his eyes. "It happens so quickly. So, so easily. But that's exactly what the devil wants."

My chest closes. I can't speak, or think, or breathe. Pressure builds behind my eyes as Father Gabriel presses his mouth into a thin line.

"We can never comprehend the full extent of God's plan. Especially if we turn our back on Him during difficult times."

Difficult times?

Sadness turns to anger. The pressure is still there, scalding my eyeballs. Moisture builds, but these aren't tears of mourning.

These are tears of rage.

Not the first I've shed. I'm sure not the last.

There are so many things I want to say to Father Gabriel right now. Bad things. Blasphemous things.

Hussy.

But I don't.

If he senses my anger, he doesn't acknowledge it.

"One last stop before lunch," he says as he sweeps out an arm. "In case you ever need to get something off your chest."

There's a small alcove a few feet away. The arched door set within has a brass crucifix hanging at eye level.

Father Gabriel opens the door, revealing darkness beyond.

He steps inside.

I can either follow or stay out here, stranded and alone. As much as I want to fade into the shadows, I'm done with being alone.

I trust Gabriel.

I know he wouldn't allow harm to come to me.

I follow him inside despite my tight chest and my pounding heart and my dry mouth.

I follow him into the darkness, and it swallows me whole.

4

TRINITY

Candles emerge from the gloom once my eyes have adjusted to the low light. They don't do a good job of illuminating this place—but there isn't much for them to light up anyway.

This is the tiniest chapel I've ever seen. The nave consists of six short pews, three a side, with a narrow aisle leading to the chancel.

The person on his knees in front of the altar seems too big and brawny for this intimate space.

Candle flames flicker as we move deeper inside.

As if sensing us, the figure in front bows his head a little deeper and slowly gets to his feet.

"My apologies for interrupting, Reuben."

The figure turns.

I thought it had been a man, perhaps another priest, but as the flames light the stranger's face, I realize he's a kid like me.

Okay, *kid* isn't the right word. Young man works better. He couldn't be more than a year or two older than me, but he's tall and broad and the darkness in his eyes doesn't come solely from this shadowy room.

He's dressed like Jasper was, but without the blazer. On him, his dress shirt skims defined muscles and his collar hugs a thick neck. The top button of his shirt is undone, and his tie slightly loosened, as if he was getting hot.

Unlike Jasper, he's handsome as hell.

I suddenly feel much too small for my age.

"Trinity, this is Reuben. He's in the same grade as you."

"Hi," I manage, although I doubt he can hear my whisper all of a yard away.

His dark eyes take me in, not changing one bit, and then fix on Father Gabriel. "She's a girl." His voice is deep, like I expected, but so melodious. The sound tugs loose a contraption that releases a million butterflies into my belly.

"Acute observation," Father Gabriel says through a laugh. "Trinity is my—"

Gabriel's cell cuts him off. He lifts a finger, sending an apologetic smile first my way, then Reuben's, before he slips out of the room to take the call.

When I turn back, Reuben's standing less than two feet away.

My heart jumps out of my chest as I stumble back.

"What are you doing here?" Reuben demands.

"Um…Going to school?"

His dark eyes scour mine. "You don't sound so sure."

I open my mouth to protest, but then I hear fabric rustling behind me.

"Reuben, child, show Trinity to the lunchroom."

I turn pleading eyes to Father Gabriel, willing him to understand the psychic message I'm yelling at him.

Don't leave me alone with this guy! He's a fucking psychopath!

But Father Gabriel just gives me a warm smile and a pat on my shoulder before saying, "Jasper should be in the lunchroom. He can show you to your first class this afternoon."

My skin itches, and I'm sure it's because Reuben's staring at me.

"Father—!"

"I'm sorry, I must go."

Reuben watches Gabriel leave then his eyes flicker back to me. He ducks his head and slips a rosary around his neck with reverential care. The wooden beads rattle as he tucks it under his shirt.

When he looks back up at me, my spine turns to ice.

Eyes like pools of frozen tar pin me where I stand. If I could have turned tail and run, I would have been scampering out of here like a mouse who's spotted a cat. And the cat was ready to pounce.

Reuben steps past me. I catch a whiff of something sweet and musky in the air he disturbs as he reaches back and grabs my wrist. I have no choice but to trot after him. It's that or have him rip off my arm. He doesn't walk fast, but big as he is, he covers a lot of ground even at his slow pace.

Reuben says nothing as he leads me from the prayer room and down the hall to the lunchroom. I catch a glimpse of Father Gabriel before he disappears around a corner. If I'd had a shred of common sense, I'd have called out to him. All he'd have to do was glance back. When he saw how Reuben was manhandling me he'd realize something was wrong.

But he doesn't look back.

Guess he's forgotten all about his newest charity case.

I watch Reuben's back the rest of the way, both mesmerized and horrified by the way his muscles move under his shirt.

How easily he could have snapped my neck back there.

No one would have seen.

No one would have known.

My skin crawls at the thought.

He pushes open the door. A wave of chaotic noise and

intoxicating smells wash over me. Reuben releases me and steps through. The door almost crashes into my face as it swings back on a hydraulic hinge. I catch it just in time. When I push it open, Reuben's disappeared into the bustle of boys moving around as they go to find their seats.

Thankfully, no one seems to notice me standing here.

The crowd thins at just the right time, creating an open channel to the far side of the room. Call it a miracle, but through some disturbance in the fabric of the universe, I spot Jasper. He's sitting at the end of one of the long benches chatting with the boy sitting opposite him.

Just another boy in a room filled with boys. But at least I know his name. At least he didn't just murder me with his eyes.

I push back my shoulders and head for the edges of the room, trying to find the most inconspicuous way to reach him.

Definitely not the welcome I was expecting.

J asper does a double-take when he sees me standing beside him. It took every bit of courage I had to walk through the bustling hall and make my way over here. Even more to detour and grab a plate of food. I was expecting some kind of buffet line, where staff in hair nets dished up whatever you wanted onto your plate. Instead, I had to grab the second-last food tray covered in plastic wrap from a nearby counter.

Today's lunch is thin stew and bread.

This place is really starting to remind me of a prison.

Jasper sits back, the hand holding his fork sagging. "What are you doing here?" he whispers furtively.

"Eating?" I grip my tray a little harder. The closest boys turn to stare at me. Those next to them look, then the next, then the next.

Everyone is watching me.

The entire dining hall is silent.

Dear Lord.

"Can you move up a little?" I ask quietly as my cheeks heat up.

"Fuck off," Jasper says under his breath, glancing askance at the kid next to him like he's embarrassed by my presence.

I grit my teeth. "Please?"

He shakes his head, keeping his eyes on his plate. I glance around in panic and spot a gap at the table next to us.

Before I get there, the gap disappears.

Now my cheeks are on fire.

It feels like every boy in this room is staring at me but when I look around no one meets my eye.

Screw this.

My nose can't go any higher into the air, so I push back my shoulders and strut down the middle of the room like I belong here.

Technically, I do. I'm a student here as much as any of these pricks. They have no right to treat me like a turd.

Despite my flaming cheeks, or the way my skin is intent on crawling right the fuck off me, I make it all the way to the other side of the room without wetting myself. I push open the door, my heart thundering in my chest as the door hisses closed behind me.

Relief is brief, but delicious. The plastic wrap has crept up at one edge of my tray, and I catch a whiff of the food beneath. It doesn't look like much, but it sure smells good enough to eat.

You can do this, Trinity Malone.

One day at a time, same as before. One day at a time, one after the other, thy kingdom come, thy will be done.

A-fucking-men.

My intention had been to eat my lunch in my room—if I could find my way back there. But I'd barely gone a yard before someone emerges from the nearest stairwell. A stocky woman at least two decades older than Father Gabriel latches eyes with me.

I smile weakly.

She frowns—*hard*.

My smile wilts. I stop dead in my tracks. She picks up her pace, the skirt of her habit snapping around her thick-set ankles.

"Just what do you think you're doing?" she demands as she storms up to me.

"Lunch?" is all I get out before the woman grabs my elbow, spins me around, and shoves me back the way I came.

I stumble into the dining hall amid a cacophony of sniggers and giggles and chuckles.

A second later, everyone's mouth snaps shut.

"Move," the woman snaps.

I start forward on instinct, but she catches me above my elbow. "Not you."

She surges ahead, stabs out a finger at the boy seated closest to the door, and drags a line to the side. "Move it, Nelson!"

The boy shoots to his feet, grabs his tray, and almost trips over his own feet in his hurry to get out of the woman's way as she drags me across the floor.

"Sit."

My ass hits the bench so hard, my teeth click.

"Eat."

The woman steps back and claps her hands. "Children, this is

Trinity Malone. She is a new student here. Each and every one of you will make sure that she understands and obeys the rules of our school, or I shall punish each and every one of you. Do I make myself clear?"

"Yes, Sister Miriam," the school choruses.

I'm staring so hard at my food I'm surprised it's not setting alight.

Sister Miriam lets out a huff, turns, and starts pacing the length of the hall. For a few minutes, there's only the sound of her shoes hitting the tiles. Then, with another slap, she barks, "Eat!"

Plastic knives and forks scrape plastic plates.

No one says another word.

No one looks up from their plate except me. And I only risk peeking through my lashes.

My heart slows from a gallop to a trot, but I couldn't eat if I'd crawled out of the desert having wandered forty days and forty damn nights.

One day at a time? I'm wondering if I could even get through the day at this rate.

Seriously, what else could possibly go wrong?

C *ASSIUS: We have a problem.*
 I tap my finger against the side of my phone, stroking my bottom lip with the other hand.

"Afternoon, Brother Zachary."

I glance up and give Simon a curt nod. Students file neatly into my class, seating themselves like a beautifully choreographed dance. My AP Psychology class is one of the smallest in Saint Amos—I only teach up to a dozen students in each grade.

I return the smattering of 'hellos' and 'good afternoons' before facing the chalkboard. "Today we'll be discussing epigenetics. Can anyone tell me—?"

My classroom door rattles. I glance back at my class.

All my students are present. It's highly unusual for a staff member to interrupt me once my lesson has begun. Word has long since gotten around how much that annoys me.

"Who is it?"

The door immediately stops rattling. Then a hesitant, high-pitched voice says, "Trinity."

She cuts off when I open the door and snatches away her

hands. Looks like she'd been pulling at the handle instead of pushing.

I tilt my head. "May I help you?"

The girl steps back, and huffs a dark curl away from her face. She's wearing street clothes and a thoroughly confused expression. "Yeah…uh…is this Psychology?"

T. Malone.

My new student.

I'd barely glanced at the memo slipped under my door this morning. My mind had been on other things. More *important* things. So much so, I'd even forgotten to assign her a seat.

I step back and wave her inside, my mind moving a mile a minute.

I'll be the first to admit I'm set in my ways. Which is saying something for someone who's turning twenty-one in a few months. A strange girl showing up at my door shouldn't have rattled me, but it did.

She stands at the front of the class, notepad clutched to her chest like a shield. A moment later, her amber eyes come back to mine, now even more confused than before.

I snap my fingers at a student in the front row and point to the chair behind my desk.

He hurries over, picks it up, and sets it by the wall.

"You're late," I say, when the girl keeps staring at me like she's had a stroke. "Don't let it happen again."

Still, she doesn't move.

"*You're* my teacher?"

I straighten as my hand drops to my side. "Were you expecting someone different, *Miss* Malone?"

As if she realized what she said, she shakes her head and hurries to her seat. There's a soft hiss as she plops down on my chair and the air leaves its pillow. Her fair skin looks even paler as her cheeks turn rosy with embarrassment.

It takes me a moment to gather my thoughts. As I turn back to the board, the text message on my phones comes back to me.

Could this be the 'problem' Cassius mentioned?

She's not wearing a uniform which indicates her presence took others—such as Sister Ruth, who runs the laundry—by surprise. Else she'd have been decked out in Saint Amos colors.

Her slim body, her poorly fitted clothes, the nervous energy vibrating through her—I put her at sixteen. But her eyes tell a different story. They're underlined with shadows, as if she hasn't had much sleep, and don't hold my eyes longer than a moment before she looks away.

Could be she's shy, but I suspect it's more a matter of her not wanting to give away more than she already has.

"Have you submitted your transcript to the administration office?" I ask, turning my back on her as I scratch out a note on the chalkboard.

"I…I don't have one."

I turn back to her, subtly aware the other students in my class are following our exchange like a particularly slow—if fascinating —tennis match. "Which school did you attend? I'll have it sent over."

"I was…homeschooled."

"Ah." I click my fingers at the student closest to her and turn back to the board. "Sit with Alex. He can share his textbook with you."

She drags her chair over to the closest table, and the boy reluctantly slides his textbook to the side so she can lean across and read with him.

Homeschooled? That's a first for Saint Amos. At least, since I became a teacher here. Most of our students are children from across the state who couldn't afford private tuition and whose parents—for whatever reason—had decided they didn't want them in a public school.

Those who still had their parents, of course.

Many students at Saint Amos are orphans.

Is that the case with Trinity Malone? If so, why isn't she at the all-girls school up in Devon? Sisters of Mercy never turns anyone away.

I glance over my shoulder. Trinity immediately drops her gaze back to the textbook, and her cheeks turn rosy again. I take in the rest of the class. Most of the boys are surreptitiously peeking over at her, some hiding the fact behind hands or raised up textbooks.

I'm fully aware of her presence through the rest of my lesson, and find myself watching her more often than my students. Perhaps it's because she's a new and shiny thing in a place usually full of shadows and cobwebs.

I need to find out what she's doing here.

If this is in fact a coincidence, then so be it. But if there's any chance she'll disrupt our plan, then we'll have to get rid of her.

The new girl doesn't have anything to pack up except her notebook. She clutches it against her chest as she makes a beeline for the classroom door. The bell is still sounding its last gong when she disappears out the door without so much as a glance in my direction.

My regular students stream out of the room, each pausing to thank me or bid me a good afternoon before they leave.

Many of them used to have abysmal grades before they joined my class last year. The devotion and passion I pour into each class are beginning to show. With my help, these boys will get a head start on their degrees.

Moments after the last student leaves my class the door opens again.

I glance up. My body tenses soon when a student slips into my class. He peeks outside before silently closing the door and turning the lock.

"What's so important it couldn't wait?" I ask dryly, straightening the things on my desk as Cassius Santos slinks closer. "And fix your fucking tie, Santos."

"You can drop the act," Cassius rests his thigh on the corner of my desk as he crosses his arms over his chest and leers at me. "It's just us."

"Hallway monitors don't mock the dress code. Or did you forget that you're supposed to be a star pupil?"

The eighteen-year-old student is tall and well put together. Stark blue eyes contrast a dark buzz cut that accentuates his features even more than a mop of hair would have. He pretends to adjust his clothes, but when he drops his hands his tie is still crooked and his top button still undone.

"Whatever," Cass mutters. "And it's not a what, by the way. It's a *who*." He stabs a thumb over his shoulder. "She just left your class."

I close my drawer and sink into my seat, leaning back and crossing an ankle over my knee. We shouldn't be meeting like this, but the other classrooms should already be empty by now— the chances of someone seeing us are slim to none.

"It's not the first time we've had a female student, or an enrollment so late in the term."

"That's what I thought." Cassius narrows his eyes to blue slits. "But then Rube came to talk to me. Told me Old Scratch was showing her around like a tour guide. He seems to think they're pretty tight."

I shrug. "I'll take a look at her file this afternoon." I grab my ankle, pressing my thumb into one of the tendons. It's an old injury, one that usually doesn't pester me this much in warm weather. Its twin on the other ankle starts aching too, but I leave it be. "If there's cause for concern, you'll be the first to know."

"What if she fucks this up, Zac?" Cass's arms tighten as he ducks down a little. "It's taken us *years* to get to this point. If she's going to be one of those closet nuns who hang around Lucifer the whole time, how are we supposed to..." he lowers his voice, leans close "...get rid of him? You told us it would only work if no one misses him for like a week. If this chick's his niece or something, don't you think she'll notice if he suddenly disappears?"

I recognize the storm brewing in Cassius's eyes. "Tell Apollo to keep an eye on her, if you're so damn worried," I say.

"Will as soon as he gets back. He's been out in the woods most of the day. Somehow managed to convince the old hag to let him leave the grounds."

My eyes shift to the window panes. They're high up on the wall, and less than a foot across each. They don't show anything of the world outside except a few pieces of the sky—classrooms are for learning, not for daydreaming. But I know this place well enough to know how far away those trees are. It's one of the things the staff of Saint Amos drill into every student who attends—no one goes past the fence. If they're caught, they're expelled.

Too many students have gotten lost in those woods, most of their bodies never recovered. Those that were? Hardly recognizable once the wild animals out there had finished with them.

Trust Apollo to charm his way into being allowed to spend the day out there. He hasn't even been here the longest. This is my second year at Saint Amos. Apollo graduated last year, and Reuben and Cassius will be graduating this year.

We made sure not to arrive at Saint Amos in the same year.

We couldn't risk anyone piecing together the fact we knew each other. That's why we've always kept our relationship on a need to know basis.

A dry chuckle escapes my lips. "Fuck my life."

"I'd rather fuck her."

My eyes snap back to Cassius. "Not a chance. You don't go near her until we know who she is."

Something flickers over Cass's face, but it's gone before I know what it means.

"Don't fuck her." I narrow my eyes at him. "In fact, don't even *look* at her."

"Aye, aye, Boss." He gives me a mock salute before leaving my classroom as surreptitiously as he entered.

My muscles loosen, but not as much as they should. If my brothers are all as restless and uneasy as Cassius, then we could be facing disaster.

But he's right—we're running out of time. And this girl could be no one...or the person who causes this web to unravel. A web we've been building for years.

My ankle throbs, but I ignore it this time.

I'm stronger now. My body doesn't have full control over me anymore.

But I don't have full control over my mind.

It was a tradeoff I was happy to make. One we've all made at some point in our journey.

That's why we stuck together. That's why we formed our brotherhood of revenge.

Alone, we were nothing but prey.

Together, we've become the ultimate predator.

Sister Stella gives me a warm smile when I step through the door to the administration office that afternoon. While Saint Amos only has two female teachers, all of the administration staff are women. Students' grades, school supplies, and everything else the school needs to run are handled from the cluster of offices on the east wing of the school's main building.

Framed by her black-and-white habit, only the center of Sister Stella's face is visible.

"Good afternoon, brother. Something I can help with?" she asks, rising from her desk.

Saint Amos has telephone lines and electricity, but everything looks like it's from the 1960s. No computers. No internet. And since the telephone lines are down more often than they work, everyone relies on their cellphones to maintain contact with the outside world.

When there's service, of course.

Certain places on campus don't get any service, like the libraries nestled deep in the disused catacombs.

Originally a church, all of the original buildings remain intact. When this place became an orphanage, the catacombs were used as an infirmary. These days, it houses the library. Unconventional, since the classrooms are a good fifteen-minute walk away, but more cost-effective than building a new structure. In fact, the low, squat building housing the classes is the newest structure on the property.

"I'd like to take a look at Trinity Malone's transcripts, if she has any. May I see her file?"

Sister Stella widens her eyes at me, and gives her head a tiny shake. "I'm sorry, brother, I only requested it this morning. We didn't even know she was coming until the provost mentioned it after prayers."

"That's strange," I say, resting my elbows on the reception desk and leaning in a little. "Why was no one notified?"

Stella shrugs. "Perhaps it slipped the provost's mind. He's under a lot of stress at the moment, what with—"

"Yes, I understand." I shouldn't have interrupted her—I'm supposed to be the kind of person who cares deeply about Father Gabriel's state of mind.

In a way, that's *all* I care about these days.

I was hoping her file had arrived already. Why did her arrival at Saint Amos take so many people by surprise? I doubt it slipped Gabriel's mind. He's the most intelligent and cunning man I've ever had the displeasure of meeting.

Her file would have told me all I needed to know. Where she came from, what her connection to Gabriel and the school is. No one just *enrolls* at Saint Amos—students have to be referred by the bishop of their diocese.

If I know who her emergency contact is, I could contact them and find out even more.

But not without her file.

And maybe that's exactly what Gabriel wanted. Maybe he didn't want anyone knowing who she is, or how she's connected with him.

Why?

"When is he leaving?" I ask, keeping my voice casual.

"Let me confirm." She lifts a finger, giving me another honey-sweet smile. Then she turns her head a little and calls out, "Sister? When does Father Gabriel leave?"

"Thursday afternoon," a voice replies from one of the rooms branching off this reception area.

"And her file?" I ask. "When are you expecting it?"

Stella turns back to me. Her shrug is nearly invisible beneath her habit. "I'll let you know as soon as it comes in. But I doubt there'll be a transcript. Probably a few report cards and her family history. She was homeschooled, you know?"

"I'm aware," I murmur. "Thank you, Sister."

How long will I have to keep Cassius in check? I refuse to make a move until I know how she fits into all of this. From the sounds of things, she was brought here by the provost himself.

I'm not okay with an innocent being caught up in the fray. We planned this so there would be no collateral damage.

Our window of opportunity is closing. Fast.

And there will never be another chance like this.

6

TRINITY

"Hey, wake up!"

I scramble to a sit, blinking hard as I try to focus.

Jasper's leaning over my cot. He's dressed in his school clothes. The last time I saw him he'd been wearing athletic shorts and a vest.

That had been yesterday afternoon.

"What time is it?"

"Didn't you hear the bell? It's breakfast," he snaps. "We all say prayers before. They won't let you lie in unless you're sick. Are you sick?"

I wish I could have convinced him I was. But the only thing wrong with me is the sudden conviction I've lost my freaking mind. I slept right through dinner? No wonder my stomach feels like a black hole.

I'd been planning to take a quick nap. After all, no one had told me what I was supposed to do after I finished Calculus, my last class of the day. Jasper must have come to bed at some stage, but I don't remember that at all.

What I *do* remember is how tongue-tied I'd been at meeting

my Psychology teacher. I guess he's not too young to be a teacher, but he's definitely too good looking. How is anyone supposed to concentrate?

Maybe that's why he chose to teach at an all-boys school.

Jasper scans my rumpled cardigan and jeans. "You can't wear that."

"Yeah, God, I know."

"You can't say that."

"You know what?" I hop off the cot, so close to him I could knee him in the groin if I wanted. And dear Lord, how I want to.

"You can't tell me what to do." I poke his chest.

"If you don't obey the rules, *I* get punished," Jasper says, tilting his head. "Think I like getting lashes? *No one* likes getting lashes." He spins around, yanks open his closet, and tears a set of clothes from one of his hangers.

I don't have time—or space—to move out of the way. He shoves the bundle of fabric against my chest so hard I stumble back and end up sitting on my bed.

It creaks.

I scowl up at Jasper.

He glares back.

"Put that on and haul butt to the chapel outside." He points at me. "And don't you dare try to sit next to me."

With that, he's gone.

I throw on Jasper's clothes and hurry into the hall but he's nowhere in sight. This hallway only has two exits, both with staircases. I pick the east side, and sprint down the hall before thumping down the stairs two at a time.

I breathe a sigh of relief when I spot Jasper turning the corner.

Jogging after him, I try and neaten my clothes on the way.

His shirt is too tight around my breasts, but not if I keep the top three buttons open and use his tie to cover my cleavage. His pants are tight around my ass. I'm hoping I can sit down without splitting them.

The outfit looks ridiculous with my ballerina pumps—there'd been no time to change those—but at least I only have to turn up the hems once so I don't step on them.

My hair is a train wreck. It's super curly on a good day, and I must have been rolling around in my sleep last night because now it's a tangled mess. Even trying to get the elastic band out of it brings tears to my eyes, so I decide to leave it in.

At least I'm wearing a uniform. Now Jasper can stop fantasizing about being whipped because I'm in jeans.

I arrive at the downstairs hallway alone with no roommate in sight.

The dining room doors are standing open.

It's empty.

Where the hell is everyone?

We all say prayers before

Shit.

In my hurry to chase down Jasper, I'd forgotten about prayers.

I'm in the wrong building.

My boobs jostle each other as I turn and sprint for one of the side doors leading out of the dormitory. I followed a group of students from the lunchroom yesterday—that's how I found my way to class. If it hadn't been for them, Jasper wouldn't be able to sit down for the lashes he'd have gotten.

What a prick.

I head for the chapel. The crucifix poking out from atop its little tower makes it easy enough to spot.

Far ahead, a handful of students hurry toward the chapel. I'm almost there when movement catches my eye. I glance over my shoulder, and stub my toe the same instant I catch sight of someone breaking away from the shadow of a nearby maple tree.

I lose sight of the figure as I hop on one foot and grit my teeth against the pain. When I look back, he's gone.

The fine hairs on the back of my neck lift up.

Someone *was* standing there. Shoulder length hair, sandy or blond, and a video camera in his hand. Not a cellphone or anything—a proper video camera with a lens.

Maybe I am hallucinating.

It wouldn't be the strangest thing to happen since I've set foot in this place. My toe aches in time with my hammering heart as I step inside the chapel.

Awe washes away the pain.

This is nothing like our church in Redmond. That place always reminded me of a converted barn. It could seat two hundred and store a bunch of hay bales at the same time.

This place?

Oh my fucking Lord.

Whoever built this place must have been blessed with visions of heaven. Maybe he'd been dying of syphilis or something. You'd have to be on the spectrum to create something this...

"Gorgeous, isn't it, Little Hussy?"

I instantly recognize the voice. It's the guy who threw me up against my closet yesterday morning.

I try to swing around. He clasps my shoulders, keeping me facing forward.

The thought of this guy touching me makes my insides clench. I should be horrified, *terrified*…but for some reason my body isn't on the same page as my mind.

His touch sets everything inside me squirming.

"You'd think it was some crazy-talented architect who built this place, wouldn't you?" His breath tickles the hairs alongside my face. "Turns out, it was just some religious nut who knew how to use a hammer."

Still rooted to the spot, I don't have a choice but to take in—I mean *really* take in—this place. Everything from the vaulted ceiling to the immaculately designed stained glass windows. The floor is a ceramic artwork of mesmerizing patterns so glossy it reflects the rows of pews like a mirror.

It must have taken years to construct.

"Better take your seat, New Girl. Old Scratch hates it when we're late to prayers."

Then he slaps my ass.

Hard.

My gasp travels through the chapel like a whip crack. Everyone turns around to look at me, some grabbing hold of the backrest of their pew to twist in their seats.

I can't imagine what I look like, standing in the doorway with my hands clutched at my chest, hair disarrayed and cheeks glowing like hot coals.

I'm not in the least surprised when most of the boys start snickering into their hands.

Moving on wooden legs, I force myself to the closest pew.

I don't bother looking behind me. I already know the guy who'd been standing there whispering into my ear like Satan himself is gone.

But he must still be watching me from somewhere, because someone's staring at the back of my head.

I take a deep breath, and let it out slowly.

At least my pants haven't split. Today might even turn out to be a good day.

It seems the first two rows are reserved for the teachers and staff. I glance at them all and try to figure out who they are.

Dressed in full clerical vestments, Gabriel strides onto the chancel. I'm so relieved to see a familiar face I'm blinking away tears.

I hope I can talk to him before school starts. I know I'm the only female student here, but for heaven's sake, this can't be normal. Maybe if he makes an announcement or something, like that other woman—Sister Miriam?—did. He can tell the boys to leave me the hell alone.

I push back my shoulders and sit up a little straighter.

But then I remember what he told me yesterday. That the boys around here earn *privileges*. I guess there's no way he'd consider showing me any kind of special treatment.

After a short sermon, Father Gabriel leads us in the Father's Prayer.

Our father, who art in heaven.
Hallowed be thy name.

I barely murmur the words loud enough to move my lips. I wouldn't be praying along at all, but I guess it won't hurt.

What else is there to do but keep playing along like I have been all my life? What's a few more weeks, months, years?

Maybe by becoming the perfect student, I'll earn myself a

private room. Perhaps even some kind of protection against the boys.

It's a lot to hope for, but I have Mom's stubbornness on my side.

I duck my head and squeeze closed my eyes. My lips tremble as I fight with myself. But this time, I lose the battle.

Thoughts pour into my mind like rancid oil.

How could you abandon me like this?

You weren't even supposed to be in that car with him.

You were supposed to be at home, with me.

You're my mother.

You told me you loved me, and then you chose him over me.

You always did.

I bite the inside of my lip until I taste copper.

I hate you.

I hate *you!*

I fucking hate—!

A hand lands on my shoulder. "Trinity?"

I jerk away from the touch, and turn brimming eyes up to Gabriel. "Father," I manage in a wobbly voice.

"May I join you in prayer?"

I'm vaguely aware of boys streaming past him in the aisle watching us intently.

If I spoke, I'd start sobbing like a kid so I scoot silently aside. Father Gabriel takes a seat beside me, his thigh warm and hard where it presses against mine. With a quick smile at me, he sits forward and rests his elbows on the backrest in front of our pew. Then he clasps his hands and bows his head.

Guilt eats through me like a heap of maggots.

He thought I was praying when he walked past, when in truth I was cursing my dead mother.

I fold down, pressing the tips of my steepled fingers to the skin between my brows hard enough to bruise. It helps with the shaking, and at least now I'm hidden behind Gabriel's figure. If the boys walking past want to gape at me, they won't be able to see much.

But even now, like this—shielded by the provost—someone's watching me.

Are they waiting for me to fuck up and expose myself as the heretic I am?

Or are they intrigued by this stranger in their midst?

Well fuck them.

Whoever they are, they can go straight to hell.

7

TRINITY

I don't bother trying to find anyone to sit with at breakfast. I hadn't even planned on going to the dining hall after the terrible time I'd had at the chapel. But on my way back to the main building, Sister Miriam makes a beeline for me and falls in step beside me.

"I trust you are keeping well, Miss Malone?"

Miss Malone.

A faint tingle works its way deep inside me. I don't know why, but my entire body came alive when Brother Zachary had spoken my name yesterday. In fact, that had happened every time he'd looked at me too.

"Yes, thank you." My voice is still thick with emotion. I don't know how long Father Gabriel and I sat praying in the chapel. It felt like hours had gone by before he shifted in his seat and let out a soft, "Amen," before excusing himself.

"What are you wearing?" Miriam asks, in exactly the same tone she'd used to greet me with.

"A uniform?" I look down at myself. My tie has shifted, exposing my cleavage.

I turn bright red. It must have been the run over here that did it. So was it like this the entire time Gabriel sat beside me in prayer?

Despite what I'd always thought, dying from shame is not only a possibility, but it seems destined to be *Miss* Malone's fate.

"Come see me after breakfast." She breaks away and heads for the classrooms.

Someone's watching me again. I scan all around me.

There's no one sight.

I stare at the distant trees. It's so dark under that dense canopy, they could easily move around on the edges of the grounds without being seen.

Goosebumps break out on my skin.

I almost get all the way through breakfast without incident. En route to the table to put down on my empty tray, I feel eyes on me again. This time I don't hesitate—I immediately scan the entire dining hall to see who's looking in my direction.

Quite a few of the boys still seated at the benches are looking my way, but they duck their heads when I make eye contact.

Except the pair at the far back of the room. There beside the table with hot water urns for tea and coffee is the same sandy-haired guy I'd seen outside the chapel.

This time there's no mistaking the video camera in his hand.

Or the fact it's trained on me. He's not looking through it. He's watching the little fold-out screen.

I hastily put my tray on top of the others. Time to get the hell out of here. My tray upsets the entire pile. I wince as the trays clatter to the floor by my feet.

Not all of them were empty.

My pants—*Jasper's* pants—are now splattered with oatmeal and runny eggs. Some of it even got in my fucking hair. On instinct, those same disastrous words start playing through my head.

It can't possibly get any worse than this.

It can't *possibly* get *any* fucking worse than this.

But it does.

Everyone starts laughing.

"Gees," someone says behind me. "Were you born under a ladder or something?"

I half-turn to Jasper, scared the ceiling might collapse on me if I make any sudden moves. "I'm sorry about your clothes."

"Yeah, me too." Jasper shakes his head. "But it's kinda impossible to stay pissed off at you."

I shake a glob of oatmeal from my hand with a sigh. "At least I got that going for me."

"You gotta take a shower." He makes to grab my elbow, but I've had about all the manhandling I can, well, handle.

I move away from him, lifting my hands. "Just tell me where it is."

He stares at me for a second, and then laughs and shakes his head. "Bet I'll hear about a busted water main in an hour or so." He shrugs. "But hey, it's your funeral."

After using the restroom on the third floor, I'd assumed the bathroom would be one of many. A private room with a tub and a shower—possibly even a combo, for efficiency—and a basin for the boys to shave in. Maybe even some stalls.

How very naive of me.

Saint Amos was *definitely* a prison in one of its earlier

incarnations. Church, prison, orphanage, boarding school. Isn't that the natural progression of places like this?

Situated on the second floor, the bathroom looks more like a locker room. On the left, a row of basins and mirrors. To the right, a wall of showers. *No* shower curtains. A low wall separates every pair of showerheads from the next.

A long bench splits the room down the middle.

Because showering with your roomie adds to the fun.

I shudder at the thought.

Where the hell am I supposed to put in my tampon? Or do I go and squat next to the bench when no one's looking?

I'm dimly aware I need to get a move on—Sister Miriam said to meet her after breakfast, and I think I have class with Brother Zachary first thing, but I'm so busy trying not to lose my shit all that stuff fades into the background.

I strip and hurry to the closest showerhead. I fully expect only cold water to come out, but after a few seconds I'm delightfully surprised by a lukewarm stream.

I slather no-name brand soap and shampoo—no conditioner, duh—over myself while I try not to think about athlete's foot. The fact this feels so good is a dire testament to how shitty the past few days have been.

As much as I'd love to stand here for a few minutes and let the warmish water batter out some of my stress, I'm pretty sure I'm tempting fate. The longer I stay here, the higher the chance someone will decide they need to shower or shave or sit down on a bench for no reason.

I dry off and put on the dress I brought with me. It's far from flattering—nothing in my sparse wardrobe can *possibly* be considered seductive—but I still feel overly exposed as cool air washes over my bare legs and arms. Even slipping on my cardigan doesn't help.

I hesitate, and then toss Jasper's dirty clothes into what I assume is the laundry basket in the corner of the room.

I wring out my hair and pat it dry with a towel as I hurry back to my room. Since I have no idea how long this thing with Sister Miriam will take, I'd rather fetch my notebook so I have it on me before Zachary's class.

I don't dare show up late to his class again.

There's an envelope on my bed.

I tear it open and pull out a class schedule typed out on a typewriter.

TUESDAY

7:00am - Prayer

7:30am - Breakfast

9:00am - English

10:00am - AP Psychology

11:00am - Free

12:00pm - Lunch

On and on it goes, spelling out every minute of my day till the last bell—lights out. I'd literally been lights out when that one rang last night.

I haven't had much time to consider how different things would be. I loved being homeschooled, but I'd never known anything else. Mother was an excellent teacher, but she'd also get into a mood sometimes and give me the day off to do what I wanted. Days like that I'd usually end up at the local library, reading whatever I could get my hands on.

Maybe structure is exactly what I need. I can just follow my schedule day after day until it becomes my new norm. No need to think.

Hopefully, by then, I'd have fooled myself into believing there could be such a thing as normal again.

I toss the towel on the foot of my bed, snatch up my notebook, and head down the hall.

I'm halfway down when the school bell tolls.

Shit! It's already nine?

I glance through one of the windows I pass, but it's impossible to make out where the sun is through the stained glass.

Who would I rather *not* piss off: Zachary, or Sister Miriam?

Since I have no idea where Sister Miriam is—does she have an office or something?—I choose Zachary.

With my dress flapping around my knees and my hair dripping water down my neck, I sprint over the grounds and hurtle into the classroom hallway.

I remember to push the door and not pull on it this time.

One point for Miss Malone, nine-hundred ninety-seven for the universe.

Brother Zachary glances at me from the blackboard. Forest green eyes narrow. His dark hair is long but carefully brushed back from his diamond-shaped face and dimpled chin.

Oh Lord, he's just as intense as I remember. And, like yesterday, my body reacts in the strangest way. Everything inside me goes tight and then, when I think I'm going to pass out from lack of oxygen, my lungs fill with air.

That breath calms me a little, despite how Zachary's face hardens when he sees me.

But it does nothing for the tingle dancing between my legs.

"Late again, Miss Malone."

My heart thumps in time with his words, as if he's controlling my organs.

If he is, then he's one cruel bastard.

Because as I force myself to walk across his classroom, it's as if he slides inside me and starts toying with my guts.

I should hate him for having such an effect on me.

Instead, all I can think about is him touching me. Not with his eyes, but with his hands.

I know I've missed out on a lot in my sheltered life.

Playdates, sleepovers, movies at the mall.

Kissing.

Sex.

I've always been intrigued by the concept. What would it feel like? Who would be the one to finally deflower me?

Against all logic, I'd resisted the thought it would be with the scrawny, pimple-faced kid from our church Mom kept trying to set me up with.

My dreams had centered around someone a lot more like Zachary. Tall and handsome and charismatic in his own way.

Maybe that's why I'm reacting like this. Since I'd started here, I've been bombarded with good looking boys.

Well, four, anyway.

I doubt I'd have felt the same way about anyone in this class. But it's not just the way they look. There's something else. At least with Brother Zachary, it's a little more obvious. He exudes a dark aura. His steely eyes, and the way he walks like he owns the room and every stick of furniture inside it.

Even the students.

Especially me.

Every time I step into this class, it's blatant I'm entering his domain, and I'm only here because he allows it.

8

TRINITY

Yesterday I spent my entire Psych lesson trying to ignore the fact I was apparently head over heels in love with my teacher. Today isn't going much better but at least I'm taking some notes.

Every time he happens to glance at me, I blush.

"…next stage, which is postnatal. Those can include neglect and *what*?"

It's the quiet that drags me from my thoughts. I've resorted to staring at my notebook and doodling circles in the margins so I won't catch on fire.

I look up.

Yup—everyone's staring at me.

What now?

Reluctantly, I look over Zachary.

He's holding a piece of chalk against the board, poised to write.

"Neglect and *what*?" He taps the chalk, dipping his head a little.

Dear Lord—he wants me to answer? My mouth opens as my

eyes take in the diagram he's drawn. This stuff all sounds very familiar. I'm sure Mom already went through this part of the curriculum, but for the life of me I can't remember anything.

"I don't know."

My heart turns to lead when disappointment darkens his eyes.

He turns and points to one of the boys. "Eric?"

"Abuse?"

Zachary says nothing, but the tap-squeak of his chalk speaks volumes as he writes down the answer.

"Thank you, Eric. Abuse and *neglect* can affect genetic change during the postnatal stage of an individual's life."

I keep my head down for the rest of the lesson, not even daring to look up when I hear silence. Unless he calls on me directly, I'm not fuck risking it.

Thankfully, he ignores me for the rest of the lesson. By the time the bell sounds, I'm such a bundle of nerves I drop my pencil twice before I can shove it into my dress pocket. It sticks out halfway, but at least it's got a better chance of staying in there than in my hand.

I try and merge with the boys leaving class, ridiculously assuming they'd provide camouflage.

Instead, I cause chaos.

Some of them step back to let me through the door first. Others, as if sensing Armageddon is seconds away, speed up so they can exit first. I end up getting bounced around like a pinball.

Zachary watches impassively, not even bothering to catch me when I stagger. For my own safety, I wait to the side until everyone's left.

"A moment, Miss Malone," Zachary says, like I knew he would.

I try and keep the door open—it's set on a hydraulic hinge

like the lunchroom—but Zachary puts his head to the side and that's somehow a command for me to approach.

The door hisses closed.

I creep closer and try to disappear behind my notebook.

"I'm not like the others," Zachary says.

A downright hysterical laugh escapes me before I can press my lips closed.

Zachary's eyes darken to the green of tree shadows as he perches on the edge of his desk. "Which part of this amuses you, Miss Malone?"

I bite the inside of my lip and hope it will be enough to stop me from losing my shit. But he waits me out, so I shake my head and try to look meek.

"Is it the part where you receive penance for continuously showing up late to my class?"

Continuously? Dude, it's the second day of my miserable stay at Saint Amos. Have a little—

"Or is it the part where you fail this class because you can't be bothered to apply yourself?"

My face heats up. I wish I could say something, but I don't trust myself to speak, especially since I still feel like laughing.

Who does he think he is? He's treating me like a ten-year-old. I can't believe I liked this guy. He's horrible.

"I only got my schedule this morning." The words are out before I can stop them.

Zachary tilts his head. My guts worm around in my belly at the intensity of his stare. "And your voice? Did that also just arrive?"

I just shake my head.

His eyes flicker away, as if he's suddenly lost his patience. He stands, steps closer. "I'll tell you again. I'm not like the others." He bends and reaches down.

He's going to touch my bare leg. Is that why he kept me back? He's so close I can make out the patterns in his irises.

His perfect skin, his expressive mouth, the tendons in his neck that tense as he stretches out his hand.

Oh, Lord, how badly I want him to touch me.

But not on my leg.

I squeeze my thighs together.

There.

That's where I want him to touch me.

Right between my—

Zachary holds up my pencil. "I don't give second chances," he says before tucking it back into my pocket. It must have fallen out when that guy bumped me. "I'm writing you up for this, and I suggest you do whatever it takes to be on time for my next class."

His words mean nothing to me. I'm hypnotized by the way his mouth moves.

"Do I make myself clear, Miss Malone?"

He's still a foot away, but I want him closer. I want to know if his touch will be gentle or firm. I imagine his large hands will demand from my body what he demands from my mind.

"Miss Malone." It's not a shout, but the snap in his voice goes right through me like he yelled.

"I'm sorry, Sir," I babble. "I promise I won't be late again."

The door whooshes open. Sister Miriam steps inside, ruddy face framed by her habit. "There you are!" Her mouth turns into a cruel curve. "Wait in the hall for me." She stabs out her finger, and my body moves without a single thought from my brain.

It's blessedly cool in the hall, blessedly quiet.

I can hear them speaking, but I can't understand a word through the closed door. I press my back against the wall and close my eyes, gathering myself with effort.

If the tingling between my legs is anything to go by, I'm

going to have a hell of a time getting Brother Zachary out of my head today.

What the hell is wrong with me? Why am I suddenly acting like a teenager with raging hormones?

Yes, technically I am still a teenager, but I've never been—

A hussy?

When Sister Miriam comes out, she looks a touch calmer than she did going in. Zachary seems to have that effect on everyone except me.

"Follow me," she says in a snippy voice.

"Uh…I have English—"

"Not today. I've already spoken with your teacher."

Miriam leads me to the main building, then through the dining hall and into the big kitchen. A few people move around the large space—I guess if you're feeding so many students, meals take hours to prepare.

There's a guy kneading bread nearby. His arms are dusted in flour up to his elbows, and his long blond hair swept under a hairnet. He looks up when we enter the kitchen, and his eyes stay on me the entire time as Miriam leads me across the floor.

There's something familiar about him, and I only catch on right before Miriam opens another door and leads me through.

He was the one with the video camera.

I turn, glancing back over my shoulder.

He's standing up straight, a smudge of flour on the tip of his nose. He'd be handsome if his features weren't so gaunt.

I hesitate, and then wave.

He gives me a smirk.

The laundry room's air smacks into me like a warm, damp towel. There are a handful of women and two younger boys in here, all drenched with sweat. Massive washers rumble along one wall. Clean linens drape a row of tables in the center of the long, narrow room.

Further down, racks of pressed uniforms stand waiting to be delivered to the boys's rooms.

"Strip," Sister Miriam commands.

I stop walking and cough like I've swallowed a fly. "Excuse me?"

She turns, clasping thick arms over her stomach. "I need to take your measurements. Ruth!"

An older woman looks up from folding a bedsheet, and hurries over.

"Did you find any?"

"Yes, Sister." Ruth detours and heads over to one of the emptier racks. Hangers clatter as she drags it closer to us on squeaky wheels. With a glance in my direction, she starts going through the clothes hanging on the rack.

"Are you deaf?" Miriam asks. "I said strip!"

I glance at the other people in the washroom. All of them have their back to me, but the two boys are staring so hard at their soapy buckets I know for a fact they'll peek over their shoulders as soon as no one's looking.

I grit my teeth and force down a swell of irritation. Fighting this won't do me any favors.

I slip off my dress and hand it to Ruth. I move my hands around to take off my bra.

"Leave it."

My skin crawls, but a quick glance at the boys shows they're still engrossed in their task.

"Turn."

I pivot on my heel, and then hold up my arms so Miriam can measure me. It's the weirdest thing—standing still while a complete stranger takes stock of how big and small you are in all the important places.

My parents raised me not to be vain, but there's no way you can sprout a pair of breasts and not stare at yourself a little longer in the mirror. I know I'm far from perfect—my hips and thighs are too large and my breasts too small in comparison. I kinda hoped they'd grow a little to balance things out but that never happened.

Invisible eyes drag over my skin again.

Not the boys. Not the other washerwomen.

I scan the laundry room.

"Got it?" Miriam says.

"Yes, Sister. But I don't think any of these will work."

"They'll have to. I can't stand seeing her walking around like this."

Their voices become white noise.

The laundry doors, like the ones on either end of the dining hall, have little windows set at eye level. I barely noticed them on the way in.

The baker is on the other side of the door. With his hair net gone, his long, sandy hair hangs in his face. He drags it away with thumb and forefinger, but it just falls forward again.

He's the one watching me.

What the hell is his fascination with me? First the video camera, now this?

I get an overwhelming urge to cross my arms over my bra, but I'm not sure if the sisters are done measuring me yet. Ignoring my reddening cheeks, I lift my chin and glare at him.

So what if he wants to look? There's not much for him to see. Just a girl in her underwear.

His lips quirk up in a smile that immediately spreads into a wide grin. He takes the first two fingers of his hand and presses them to his lips. Then he touches them to the glass.

I stiffen. In a blink, he's gone.

"Turn around," Miriam says in a long-suffering voice. "Arms up all the way."

They slide a shift over my head. It's at least two sizes too big for me, and comes to mid-calf. The armholes expose the side of my bra, and the belt is two inches lower than I'm assuming it should be.

"Good gracious, this is the closest you have?" Miriam asks Ruth.

"She's a tiny little thing," the sister replies.

"Well, she can't walk around in those whorish clothes of hers anymore."

Whorish...?

I turn stunned eyes on Sister Miriam, but she's glaring so hard at the shift, she doesn't seem to notice.

Then again, they're all wearing habits.

Wait...

"Do I have to wear a habit?" I whisper.

I hope they don't hear the horror in my voice. Ruth shakes her head, lifting a finger to tut me. "No, no. There's a school dress. We just haven't made many of them."

Thank. *Heavens.*

"Bring the dress."

Lo and behold, there *is* a girl's uniform for this place.

It's brown.

It's hideous.

And it looks like they made it out of felt. I can already tell it's going to be scratchy as all hell. I take a step back before I can force myself to hold still and let them slide it over my head.

Yup. I look like a turd.

I peek over my shoulder, but there's no one by the window.

Is it weird I'd rather let that guy see me in my underwear than in this monstrosity?

"You come back here this afternoon," Miriam says, slipping a pale belt over my waist and yanking it tight.

"Oh, I won't have it ready by then, Sister," Ruth protests.

"Not for the dress." Miriam turns me around adjusts my dress as if she can somehow make it two sizes smaller by tugging it here and there. Her eyes fix on me. "This is where you'll spend your afternoons."

I open my mouth, but from the look on Miriam's face, I know there's no reasoning with her.

"Yes, Sister," I manage.

Lord, I've *got* to start earning some brownie points with Father Gabriel. I don't know how else I'm going to survive this place.

9

TRINITY

My other teachers are mostly middle-aged men and women, none of whom are even remotely as interesting as Zachary. My mind drifts in each of their classes, and it's increasingly difficult to bring it back to the subject at hand.

The dress has given me a rash along my collarbones. I scratch the rest of my body as surreptitiously as I can, but I'm sure everyone in my class thinks I have leprosy.

For the first time since I arrived at Saint Amos, I'm relieved when the bell gongs for lunch.

I don't bother trying to find Jasper—he made it clear he'd rather stick a fork in his eye than spend any more time with me than he has to. I head for the first open seat I see.

As luck would have it, I recognize the boy sitting opposite me a few minutes into my meal of sausages, gravy, peas, and mashed potato. He doesn't look like he's going anywhere, so I might as well get some answers.

"You're Jasper's friend," I say, pointing at the kid with my fork.

He leans back from me as if he's worried I'll reach over and stick him with my cutlery. "Yeah, so?"

"So what's his problem? I mean, is he genuinely just a prick, or did I do something shitty to him a previous life?"

Jasper's friend watches me with owlish eyes. "He...he doesn't like girls."

"No one in this place does." I stab a stray pea and shove it in my mouth, bursting it between my teeth. "Tell me something I don't know."

His friend shakes his head, and then ducks down.

I'm all hot and cold inside. I so badly want to thump my fist into the table and make his friend look me in the eyes. I've got a bad temper sometimes, but I never let it show back home. I'd rather suppress it until I'm alone.

Things are always easier to handle when you're alone.

"What's your name?" I ask, switching to a softer voice.

Jasper's friend glances up at me, and then shifts in his seat as if even that question makes him uncomfortable. "Perry."

"Perry...I'm going to level with you." I put down my fork and place my palms on the table, spreading out my fingers. It helps me keep calm, and Perry can see I'm not palming a switchblade or something. "I've had a horrible few weeks. I..."

Why is this so difficult?

Come on, Trinity. Just open your mouth and—

"My parents died. Recently."

Perry's eyes go even wider.

"This place is all I've got left. I'm not picking a fight with anyone. Why would I? That would just make my life miserable."

Perry nods a little.

"So why is Jasper treating me like his enemy?"

Perry picks up a pea and presses it against his lips, but he doesn't eat it yet. "Because you're a girl."

"Bullshit."

Perry shrugs.

"So he just straight-up hates all girls?"

I sit back. Perry looks relieved as he pushes the pea into his mouth and swallows.

"How can I show him I'm not a bad person?"

Perry shakes his head. Eats another pea. I pick up my fork, toying with it. "Nothing, huh?"

"I guess…"

I sit forward. "Tell me."

"I mean…he's getting really bad grades for English Lit. And you're like two grades up. Maybe you can teach him? I tried, but I'm not good at explaining stuff."

I have no idea if I *can* teach anyone anything. Then again, I've never tried. It can't be all that difficult, right? And since I don't have a clue what I'm going to do with myself after I graduate, I guess staying here for a year or two to teach would give me time to figure things out.

If I can convince Jasper to let me help him.

That's going to be the hardest part of all.

Gravel crunches under my shoes. With no moon out tonight, this path is as dark as those heading toward the stables and sports ground. This time of night, the students and staff should all be snug inside their beds.

There's a light fixture outside the crypt, but the bulb's been busted for months. The tomb isn't exactly a place students care to go, and even the staff avoid it. Superstition, of course. The only corpses nearby are those in the handful of graves outside in the cemetery.

Warm light spills out when I open the door. Should someone happen to glance out of a window, they could see me enter, but hopefully I wouldn't be recognizable.

It's one of many reasons I chose this place for our meetings.

The crypt's interior is cool and, despite the size of the room, stale.

A double row of columns cut the room in half, forming a square in the center where they meet the second row of columns intersecting diagonally.

I don't know who would ever hold a class or an impromptu

sermon in this place, but if they did, it appears the maximum seats allowed would be no more than the dozen inside that sunken square.

Twelve seats

Twelve apostles.

Only three of those seats are taken.

Apollo chuckles as he leans forward, turning his video camera so Cassius can see the playback screen. Reuben's watching the entrance. He sits up even straighter when I enter the square.

The smell of weed hits my nose.

"Christ, I almost feel sorry for her," Cass says, and then glances up at me. "You took your time, Boss. Everything okay?"

"Never better," I say as I sink down in the seat closest to Cassius.

"Apollo taped her," Reuben says, his voice steeped in disapproval.

"That was the plan." I hold out a hand for the camera.

"I didn't know why she went in there," Apollo drawls through a grin as he passes the camera to me. "Would've tried for a better shot if I had."

Him and Cassius laugh at this. I turn the camera.

Trinity's a blip on the small screen until Apollo moves closer with his camera.

I flip the screen closed without bothering to watch more.

Apollo throws up his hands. "You missed the best part."

I hold up the closed camera. "This is not what I meant."

"You said t' watch her. This is me watching her."

"Showering?"

Any normal guy might have dropped his eyes at this point. Apollo's grin grows wider. "She did a good job. I'm sure there wasn't a single spot she—"

As soon as I move my gaze from Apollo's eyes, he cuts off. With a huff, he slumps in his chair and runs his hands through his hair, unsuccessfully tucking the bulk of it behind his ears. He's almost twenty-two, but you'd think he's the youngest of the Brotherhood.

I stare at each of my brothers in turn.

"She's not a threat."

"You saw her file?" Cass sits forward, a blunt dangling from his fingertips. "What does it say?"

Sister Stella had sent a message for me this afternoon. Trinity's file had been faxed through.

From her social worker.

Trinity Malone was an orphan, like I'd suspected. Homeschooled by her parents since she was a kid, her file only had a few report cards and some very basic details. Addresses, contact numbers, that kind of thing. All useless, since both her emergency contacts were now deceased.

No referral. No indication why she'd ended up here at Saint Amos.

"Someone wants us to think she's a nobody."

Cass and Apollo groan. Reuben says quietly. It takes a lot for him to involve himself in a conversation.

"If there's some kind of relationship between her and Gabriel, the file doesn't mention it."

"We're doin' this?" Apollo asks, his voice warbling with nerves. Putting his camera down by his feet, he shoves his hands under his armpits and narrows his eyes at me.

I flick my fingers at Cass, and he passes me the blunt. I glance at each of them in turn as I hit it, diagnosing their mental states best I can.

I'm a year into my psychology major. The human psyche has fascinated me ever since I realized how fucked up a person could be.

Or, become.

Nature versus nurture.

We need to have our shit together before we act. Asking my brothers straight out if they're of sound frame of mind will earn me anything from the unvarnished truth to a flat out lie. But I've known them for fifteen years. We're brothers through and through. I can read them like I read scripture—cutting through all the bullshit metaphors and anecdotes, straight to the bone.

"You're wrong. She *is* somebody," Reuben says, as soon as my gaze settles on him.

He could put any of us on the ground in a heartbeat. But he's always been cautious. Sometimes too cautious for his own good, just like Apollo does shit without thinking things through.

Cass and I, we're somewhere in the middle. Sometimes cautious, sometimes rash.

"Why?" I say.

"He's known her a long time."

I don't even try and second guess him. Honest to God, I wish Reuben would join my psych class. What he understands on an intuitive level about most people, it would take me years to learn. Maybe it's because he listens before he speaks. He's the one that put us onto Father Gabriel in the first place, through a happenstance meeting at one of the provost's parishes.

For close to a decade, we'd been chasing a ghost. After Reuben met Gabriel in person. Then our ghost suddenly had a name and a face.

"Don't mean she's—" Apollo begins.

Reuben doesn't even pause. When he speaks, he doesn't allow himself to get interrupted. "He treats her like family."

Everyone tenses up at that.

Everyone.

Gabriel doesn't have any family. DNA like his isn't meant to be passed on. God only knows what evil his offspring would bring to this world. If he ever knocked up some chick, she'd give birth to a two-headed goat.

There's a pause while everyone makes sure Reuben is done. Then Apollo sits forward in his seat and clicks his fingers at me. I pass him the blunt without taking my eyes from Rube. "Nothing in her file indicates that he even knows her."

But, like Rube, I'm convinced that's intentional.

"If you saw what I did, you wouldn't think she was so fucking special," Apollo says in a tight voice as he passes the blunt to Cass. When he continues, smoke leaks from his lips. "That hag stripped her down like she's one of those window dolls." Apollo gestures with long hands and spindly fingers. "Wasn't being polite about it, neither."

"Get that on tape?" Cass passes the blunt to Rube, but the guy ignores him.

"Nah, man. I was working." Apollo scratches his arm. "Guys don't like it when I film them in the kitchen."

"'Cos then we'd all know who spits in our food," Cass says through a smirk.

Apollo barks out a laugh.

I'm still watching Rube. And he's watching me.

"Even if she's his fucking daughter," I say, "how could she fuck this up for us?"

Reuben shrugs—an impressive gesture on a guy with his shoulders. "We can't risk it. This is the last chance we get."

"Exactly!" Apollo's foot starts tapping. "It's our fuckin' last chance. We don't do this, we've got shit. Nothing. Fucking *nada*."

"Relax," Cassius murmurs, handing the blunt back to Apollo. "We'll figure this out."

Apollo's right. For once, time isn't on our side.

I make eye contact with Cass. He's watching me with such intensity I already know what he's going to say.

"We have to try." Cass stands. "Even if it's a fuck up. Even if we get outed, this ends with him, one way or the other."

"Sit down," I murmur.

"You knew this day was coming."

"Sit. Down."

He does, but with ill grace and the type of sulky mouth I'd expect on Apollo.

Rube's staring a hole through my head. I prop my elbows on my knees and lace my fingers together. My ankles are starting to throb, but I don't want to draw attention to the fact by rubbing them.

"Then I vote yes." I glance aside at Reuben when he remains silent. "Got to be unanimous, brother."

Reuben's chair creaks when he shifts his weight. Apollo and Cass finish the blunt between them in the time it takes him to speak. When he finally looks up at me, determination gleams in his eyes.

"No," he says.

I only realize I was holding my breath when it streams out of me in a hiss.

No.

Of course not.

Reuben doesn't take chances. If there's the smallest chance something could go wrong, he backs off.

Apollo springs up. "Jesus *fucking* Christ." He stalks out of the crypt.

Cass lets out a sigh, picks up Apollo's camera, and shrugs at us before trotting out after him.

Silence filters down between Rube and me for long minutes before I let out a sigh and rub my eyelids. "Sure about this?" I ask quietly.

"Of course," Reuben says. "She's…"

"What, Rube?" My next sigh is exasperated. "What is she?"

He taps his thumbs against the side of his knees and then slowly looks up at me. "She's one of us."

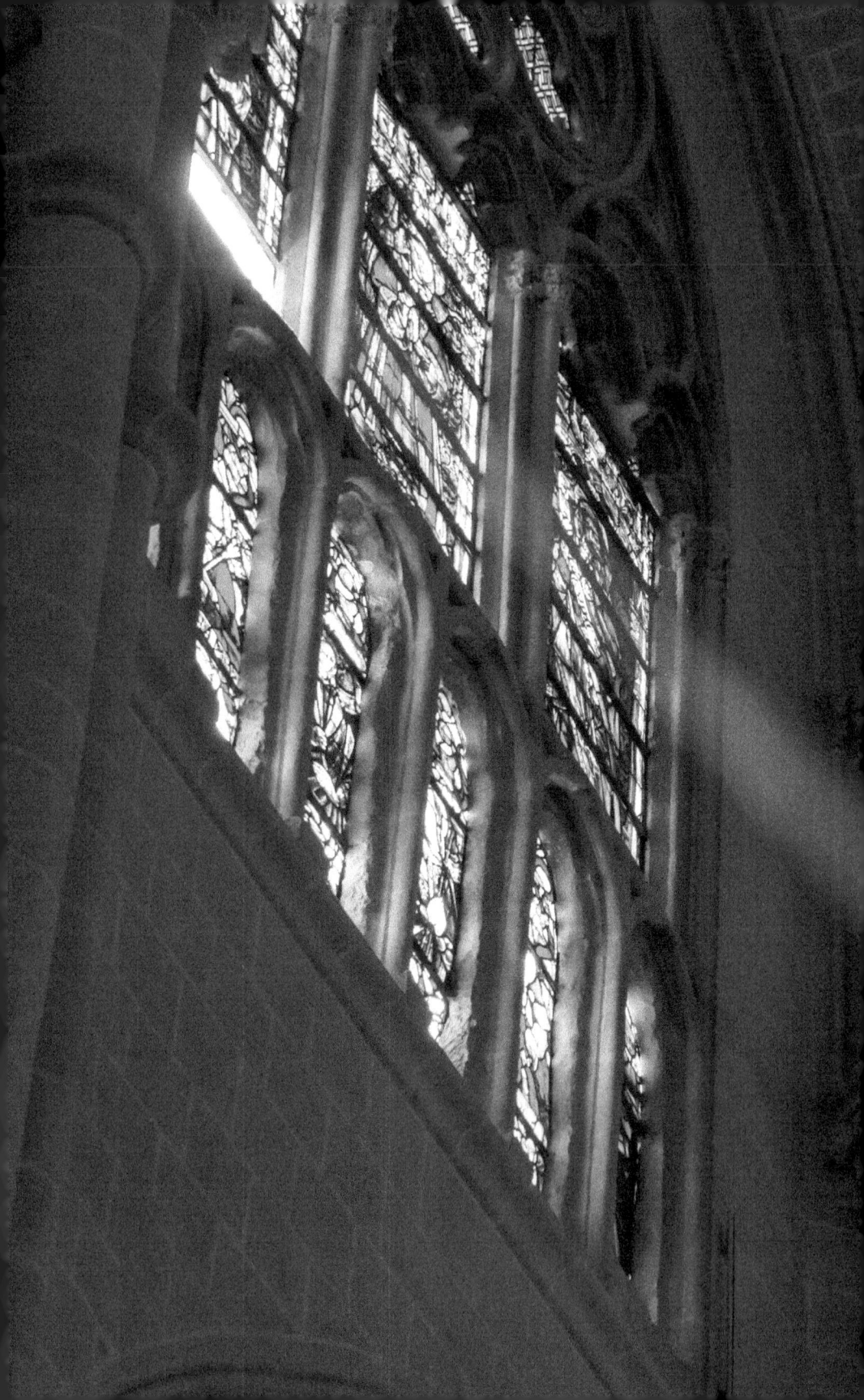

11

TRINITY

I make sure I'm awake before the first bell rings. While I was slaving away in the laundry yesterday afternoon, I had a lot of time to think.

I meant what I said to Perry.

This place *is* all I have.

So I've got to make this work. Fuck knows how, but if I'm going to spend a good three or four years here, I need to make peace with the natives.

Starting today.

I run a hand through my curls as I sit up in bed. It was too cold to sleep in my usual pajamas—cotton boxers and a vest—so I put on a sweater before crawling under the covers.

Jasper shoves away his blanket with a groan and then swings his legs over the side of the bed and yawns. When he sees me staring at him, he freezes.

"What?" he snaps, going to get his clothes from his closet.

"Did I tell you I'm thinking about becoming a teacher?"

Jasper scratches his hip without answering. He yanks out a pair of clothes and tosses them to the bed. I guess he's not going to shower this morning. Though, from the smell of sweat rolling off him, he really should.

I'd still love to know what he did to get himself stuck with me as a roommate. But that'll come in time. Right after I turn him into my BFF.

"Thing is, I was homeschooled," I go on as I start untangling my curls with my fingers. "I've never really had anyone to practice on."

Jasper's shoes thump to the floor, and he slips them on without bothering to put on socks first.

"Boo for you," he mutters, and exits the room in his trunks and vest.

I guess he's used to the cold.

"Fuck," I mutter to myself.

Guess he's not a morning person. Well, at least I planted the seed. I'll try again at breakfast.

Should I shower before school starts?

Jasper left the door open. Half-dressed boys of all ages stream this way and that across the hall, some with towels slung over their shoulders.

I sniff at my pits and shrug. At least I don't smell as bad as Jasper.

Father Gabriel leads us in prayer at the chapel. Since I got here early, I had my choice of seats. I didn't want anyone creeping up on me again, so I'm sitting near the front. This way Gabriel can watch over me.

But as soon as the provost is done addressing the school and reading today's scripture, he walks off stage. Not even a glance in my direction. It's like he's forgotten all about me.

I hesitate for a second, and then hurry after him before I can second guess myself. I hope this isn't a restricted area, because I need to know what I can do to earn my own room. And a proper school uniform. One that doesn't come pre-installed with lice.

I push open the door Gabriel disappeared behind and walked right into him.

"Trinity?" He frowns at me, and for just a second there's something very unfriendly in his eyes.

"Father. I'm—I'm sorry to just—"

His eyes soften from wood to velvety chocolate. "Gracious, I've been so caught up, I haven't had a chance to check in with you." He grabs my arm and leads me to a nearby table with a set of chairs. "How are you, child?"

I sink down, but he remains standing, forcing me to crane my neck to look up at him.

"It's been an adjustment," I admit. I was going to honey coat it—no use complaining when I'm trying to show him how well I can adapt—but he's always had a way of drawing the truth out of me.

Did he have that same effect on Mom and Dad? Did they tell him things without wanting to?

Bad things?

Sinful things?

I push away the thought. This place is making me jump at shadows. How can anyone stand it?

"I would imagine so. Tell me, how are you finding the classes? Have your teachers been accommodating?"

Teachers.

Of course! That's my way in.

"That's actually why I'm here." I twist my hands in my lap and force out the words before I can lose my nerve. "Is there a chance, I mean, do you think I could try and…?"

"You may speak freely, child," Gabriel says. He shifts his weight, looking for all the world as if he could stand there all day while I fought my tongue.

"I want to be a teacher."

He nods, waits.

"I'd like to teach here when I've finished high school. Is that...would that be...?"

Gabriel cups my face in a hand. I start at the intimate gesture, but I don't pull away. The last thing I want is to offend him. His usually vacant smile deepens. It's not the first time I've seen his dimples, but I can't remember when last he looked so happy.

"You truly are a remarkable girl."

Pressure wells behind my eyes. I drop my eyes, but he keeps me looking up with that gentle pressure on my jaw. His hands are warm, slightly calloused—which is strange for a man of the cloth. "Is that a yes?"

"I would love nothing more," he says.

He turns to leave, and then pauses and turns back. "I'll send someone to collect you tonight."

I was in the process of standing. My knees lock, leaving me in a weird half-crouch. "Uh...why?"

"We shall have dinner. God bless, Trinity."

I almost manage to reply.

Almost, but not quite.

12

TRINITY

Morning prayers ran shorter than yesterday. Despite my meeting with Father Gabriel, I get to the dining hall way ahead of everyone else. Since I don't know when Jasper's arriving, I decide to lurk in the corner close to the urns and have a cup of coffee. Which means I'm alone with the blond-haired film student when he wheels out a trolley full of breakfast trays.

At first, he doesn't see me.

The coffee must give me a spark of courage, because by the time he's done unpacking the food trolley, I march across the hall and come up behind him.

I open my mouth, but he beats me to it.

"Nice dress," he drawls. "Really brings out your eyes."

I freeze to the spot. Nice *dress*? This fabric is so stiff I could prop it up in my closet—no need for a hanger.

"Why do you keep filming me?"

"Filming you?" He turns, watching me for a second from the corner of his eye. I take back what I said before—he *is* handsome, perhaps because of his sharp nose and blade-like cheekbones. It makes him look like a fox, especially when he narrows his honey-brown eyes. "Now why'd I do that?"

"That's what I'd like to know."

"D'you really think you're that pretty?" He sets down the tray he was holding and turns to face me. When he steps forward, I step back on automatic. "Or are you just that vain?"

Now I'm regretting walking over here. I thought I'd have the upper hand, but—

Without warning, the guy tucks a stray curl behind my ear. When his fingertips brush my cheek, they leave behind a static charge that's both terrifying and exhilarating.

"Stop filming me or I'll report you."

The guy narrows his eyes again. "Who you gonna tell?"

My mind scrambles to the scariest person in this place. "Sister Miriam," I say, jutting my chin into the air. "She won't stand for it."

"What if she's the one who told me to film you in the first place?" He reaches for me again, and this time I take two steps back.

By now, boys are starting to file into the dining hall. Thankfully, one of them is Perry. The blond guy glances toward the doorway and then back at me. "I got work to do, pretty thing," he drawls through a wicked smile. "I'll catch hell if you distract me much longer."

He hurriedly offloads the rest of the trays and pushes the trolley away without looking back. I start after him, but then stop. I don't have the guts to demand his name. I mean, I barely stood my ground.

I grab a tray and hover around the table until Perry comes up to get one too. He spotted me from the doorway already. When he gets close, he moves around like a skittish deer, as if he's convinced I'm going to go for his throat.

"Morning!"

He flinches. "Hey."

"Sleep well?"

"What do you want?" he asks, frowning at me as he grabs a tray and steps back. Did I look like that when I was dodging the blond-haired guy? Like a nervous rabbit facing off with a wolf?

I'm such a wuss.

Here I am, minutes after the provost tells me how remarkable I am, and I can barely hold a conversation?

Screw that.

I've been in the passenger seat for way too long while some anonymous driver takes me from point A to point B. Time to take the wheel.

"I wanted to thank you," I tell him.

He glances back warily when I trail him to his seat. I sit beside him before he has a chance to object, and a moment later another kid boxes him in on the other side.

"What for?"

"I really think I can help Jasper." I lay my hand on top of Perry's. "I want to help him. And if I can, and he passes, then he's got you to thank for it."

Perry stares at me for a second as if I've totally caught him off guard.

"What the hell are you doing here?"

Perry snatches away his hand and ducks his head. I turn and beam up at Jasper. "Waiting for you, silly." I point at the empty space opposite us. "I want to talk to you about something."

Jasper growls out something that could have been a curse—was definitely a curse—but he sits anyway, wincing the last inch of the way as if he can't bear the thought of spending breakfast with me.

"So talk," he says, taking a noisy sip from his cup without making eye contact.

"I need a student to tutor. Do you know anyone that needs help?"

Jasper frowns at me, and then moves that look to Perry. "No," he says. "Ask the teachers."

"Oh, right!" I snap my fingers and point at him. "Of course. Why didn't I think of that?"

Because I don't want to try and teach just any kid. Jasper doesn't like me, but he seems bright enough. I want to show Father Gabriel I can do this so I'll aim for some low hanging fruit first. Plus, if I can get him to stop treating me like shit while I'm still his roommate, it would make my life that much easier.

Two birds, one stone.

Jasper scrapes his spoon through his oatmeal for a few seconds. I slurp at my coffee and take a bite of my toast, happy to shut up and wait.

I don't think he's going to go for it, when he suddenly asks, "Will it get me out of swimming practice?"

"Will what?" I ask through a mouthful of toast. I know I'm pushing it, but I need him to think this is his idea.

"Extra classes."

"What, for you? You need extra classes?"

"You said you need practice."

"I do." I drop my toast and dust my hands. "Yeah, I guess I could do a few with you. Just while I figure things out. What do you need help with? Is it math? I could def—"

"English," Jasper cuts in.

I nod, frowning a little. "Okay. Let's do it." I hold out my fist.

He stares at it until I put it back in my lap. "See you at three," he says.

I salute him with my mug of coffee.

And that, ladies and gentlemen, is how it's done.

I don't risk pissing off Jasper by joining him at lunch. Instead, I sit off to one side and munch on a slightly soggy cheese and tomato sandwich while I steal glimpses at the rows of boys. Sister Miriam pops in on our meals as randomly as if she's doing a spot check. The boys seem to have developed a sixth sense around it. Seconds before the dining room doors or kitchen doors swing open, the entire hall hushes.

As soon as Miriam's walked up and down a few times, she leaves. Seconds later, noise levels return to normal.

Maybe I *can* get the hang of this place. It can't be that hard—not if all these boys manage to coexist.

I don't have Psych today, and that suits me fine. If I did, I'd probably sprain my ankle on the way to Zachary's class and arrive late...again. Heaven knows what penance he'll assign me.

Is he the kind of teacher that would go old school and draw me over his knee? I don't think that shit's allowed anymore, but Jasper didn't look like he was kidding about getting lashes.

I head to my room just before three. I don't want Jasper to wait for me in case he loses his nerve and bails on our first lesson. Honestly, I'm a bit nervous. I paid close attention today in each of my classes, trying to figure out if there was anything specific I needed to do if I was going to start teaching. But nothing really jumped out at me, so I'm going into this blind.

"Not here," Jasper says as soon as he steps into the room.

"Oh, okay." I stand up, my notebook and math textbook pressed to my chest. "Then where—?"

"Library." He flicks his fingers, and I follow him.

He leads me out the building and across the grounds. I slow down when I realize where he's headed.

"That's where the library is?"

"Relax. It's not haunted or anything."

"But…"

Who in their right mind puts a library in a cemetery? Thankfully, our path doesn't lead us too close to the gravesides, but it's still eerie having to walk within sight of the gravestones.

The inside of the crypt is emptier than I thought. There are some chairs in the center, as if this place is used for bible study groups or AA meetings. Most of the space is filled with columns.

He leads me to the back of the enormous room and then down a circular stairwell. When I clear the stairs, I pause for a second to gape.

This chamber is huge. It's not in a cross shape like the crypt, so I'm pretty sure it extends beyond the upper building's walls.

I guess they didn't have enough dead bodies to put in here, so they decided to use it as a library instead.

Row upon row of books line the walls and form narrow aisles. Closer to the stairwell are two sections with overstuffed chairs and sofas for people to read or study. A few feet away is a podium with a large, leather-bound bible on it. A spotlight set in the ceiling illuminates it. Dust motes disturbed by our presence catch fire in that beam of light.

It's so quiet down here.

As if the books are all waiting for something…or someone.

I guess the only thing a book ever wants is to be read. It's sad to think no one ever comes down here—that's obvious by the film of dust on everything and the staleness in the air. If I ran a place like this, I'd make sure it was clean and filled with curious minds.

"We've only got an hour," Jasper says.

"Sorry." I run my hands down my thighs, grimacing at the touch of the coarse fabric. "Just…taking it all in."

He takes a seat on one of the couches and leans back, watching me expectantly. "Do that on your own time."

I roll my eyes as I take a seat on the chair closest to him.

Lord, I hope this isn't a big waste of time.

13

TRINITY

I'm in the laundry room, suds up to my elbows, when a boy comes inside and walks straight up to me. He's young, perhaps no older than thirteen.

"Father Gabriel is looking for you," he says.

"Now? I thought he said I'm having dinner with him."

The boy frowns at me. "It *is* dinner."

I must have lost track of time. There's no bell until six again, and the last one signaled the end of my lesson with Jasper. I snort quietly to myself as I flick suds off my arm and start rolling down the sleeves of my dress.

Lesson?

What a joke.

Teaching Jasper had been like trying to talk to a tree. He moved about like he had ants in his pants, but from his jaw-cracking yawns, it was obvious nothing was sinking in.

I called it quits after forty-five minutes.

"I need to change," I tell the kid as he leads me out of the laundry.

"He said to bring you straight up."

Lord, is everyone in this place missing a screw? I guess after following orders for so long you forget the meaning of independence.

Whatever. It's not like Father Gabriel would actually care what I look like. And after two hours in the laundry, I smell more of suds than sweat. I wipe my hands on my dress, hoping enough of the scent will soak into the fibers to last through dinner.

As the kid leads me up flight after flight of stairs, I take down my hair and try to get it to conform. I can only hope it doesn't look like a rat's nest.

The kid takes me to the fourth level of the building where the doorways are spaced several yards apart. The lighting is better, the floors are carpeted, and it doesn't smell like a bunch of boys crammed into a shoe closet. While my room is on the east wing of Saint Amos, Father Gabriel's is on the west.

The kid leaves me in front of a wide, arched doorway with a brass plaque:

PROVOST

No name? Guess the position suffers from high turnover.

"So do I knock, or—?"

But the kid's already gone. I push back my shoulders, paste on a smile, and knock.

No one answers.

I knock again.

No answer.

Maybe I'm too late. He could have decided to go and have dinner with the rest of the staff.

Where *do* Zachary and the rest of the faculty have dinner? Do they take their plates to their rooms, or is there a separate dining room for the staff?

On my third knock, a muffled voice calls from inside. "Come."

I turn the handle and step into a small antechamber. There's an umbrella stand, a table with a set of keys in a bowl, and a small stool beside two pairs of shoes. A second door opens into a living area.

A multitude of candles flickers as I push the door closed behind me. Polished mahogany gleams, and thick carpets eat the sound of my footfalls.

Father Gabriel is sitting in front of a fireplace on the far side of the room. There's a footstool in front of him, and he has his socked feet propped on it.

Cigarettes, wood smoke, and candle wax cloy the air, making my eyes water.

He's wearing a white t-shirt and dark jeans. Nothing like the cable-knit sweater and slacks he greeted me in on Monday morning.

He glances at me over his shoulder, and beckons. "You came straight from the laundry?" he asks as I approach.

There's a cigarette in one hand, and he flicks it against the edge of a glass ashtray without looking. He's been a smoker as long as I can imagine. Mother would never let him smoke inside our house, though. Even Dad had to smoke outside on the porch.

"Bit late to be working down there, isn't it?" he adds before taking a drag from his cigarette.

Of course I could tell him I lost track of time. But I'd rather he think I'm an overachiever than a daydreamer.

"I thought I'd stay a bit longer. They really appreciate the extra pair of hands down there."

Gabriel nods, his smile fading a little as he turns his attention back to the fire. There's a wine glass on the side table beside his ashtray—ruby liquid swirls as he brings it to his lips.

"Care for something to drink?"

"I...uh...yeah. Sure." Wine? He's giving me wine? My parents never let me drink.

Gabriel crushes out his cigarette in the ashtray and then stands and heads over to the corner kitchenette. I take a moment to scan the room as I sink into the other chair.

The heat tightens my cheeks.

I hope I don't have to sit here for much longer. Else I won't be reeking of suds anymore.

Gabriel returns with a soda can. I take it with a nod as I purse my lips. Of course the provost won't give me alcohol. What the hell am I thinking?

I crack open the can and take a sip. "It's hot in here."

"We'll move in a moment."

I glance at him from under my lashes. He sounds like his mind is miles away. I guess someone like him spends a lot of time thinking about God, even though he probably has Him on speed dial.

I look down at the can, and do my best to shove away the unpleasant thoughts trying to infiltrate my mind.

"So, uh, I hope you don't mind, but I took some more initiative today."

"Hmm?" Gabriel says, his eyes still locked on the flames.

"You know my roommate, Jasper?"

Gabriel's head snaps to the side. His vague smile is frozen on his face, but there's no mirth in his eyes. "What about him?"

My tongue tangles.

What the hell?

"Oh, he...I mean...I was tutoring him. English. We had our first lesson today."

Gabriel's eyes flicker over my face. Why do I get the feeling he's trying to catch me out in a lie? I take another sip of soda. "That's...that's okay, right? You said—"

"Oh, of course, child." His smile thaws and even spreads a little wider. "I just hadn't expected you to begin so soon."

"Should I stop?"

"Not at all." Gabriel turns back to the fire. "That boy could use a positive influence in his life. You'll do him a world of good."

Just what the hell did Jasper do? I've got to get it out of him. Maybe Perry knows.

There's a faint knock from the hallway. I'm not surprised Father Gabriel didn't hear the first two—the sound is so muffled it could be lost in the crackle of a burning log.

"That would be our supper," Gabriel says, sounding downright cheery at the concept. He stands and extends an arm as he calls out, "Come!"

I know I shouldn't stare. I know it's wrong to even have a single thought about Gabriel's body. But it's impossible not to.

For one, I hadn't expected him to be so well built. His biceps strain against his shirt sleeves, and his forearms are corded with muscles. Now his hands look proportional—his meaty palms and thick fingers a testament to a strong, fit man.

I hurry over to the table, desperate to keep my curiosity in check. Gabriel follows. I hesitate about which of the two seats to take until Gabriel pulls one out for me.

Why does this feel like a date? Then again I wouldn't know what a date was if it hit me on the head.

I thump into the seat, and drag it under the table. With my hands on my lap and my head down, I feel like I'm waiting for him to start a sermon.

Instead of cracking open a bible, Gabriel takes his seat opposite me and lays his serviette over his lap.

The antechamber's door opens. I turn on automatic.

When I see who's standing in the doorway, my blood runs cold.

R euben enters Father Gabriel's apartment with a large, covered tray in his burly arms. At first he stares at something only he can see, but as soon as he notices me, it's like I'm the only person left in the entire world.

I've never had someone look at me like this before.

It's unnerving.

And provocative.

Every nerve ending in my body switches on.

That look must only last a second, but it feels like an eternity that Reuben and I lock eyes. Then he drops his gaze, and it's as if I've ceased to exist.

"Thank you, child," Gabriel says as Reuben sets down the tray between us.

Reuben lifts the lid and goes to put it down on the counter in the dinette area. "Do you need anything else, Father?" he asks in his deep, melodic voice.

Gabriel waves at him. "That'll be all for now, child. Come back later to collect the dishes."

Reuben turns to leave, and Gabriel stands to dish up food

from the set of small dishes on the tray. I'm watching Reuben's back so I don't notice at first Gabriel is dishing up for me.

"You're looking a little thin, Trinity," Gabriel says. "Though I'm sure the past month has played havoc with your appetite."

"What?" I look down at my plate. There isn't room for another pea. "Wow...that's a lot of food."

"Your mother used to lose weight whenever she was upset. I can't remember how many pies I brought to your house, hoping to get her appetite started."

I don't remember any pies.

Reuben's walking even slower than before, as if he's listening to our conversation. It makes me want to yell at Gabriel to shut up. I don't want Reuben to know anything about me. He made it clear he thinks I'm up to no good. He'll use anything he can against me.

Even my dead parents.

"My first class was a success," I rattle out.

It was the first thing I could think of, and the worst choice of words. Today was the furthest from a success. Hopefully Gabriel isn't exactly going to interview Jasper about my teaching skills any time soon.

"Is that so?" Gabriel returns to his seat as Reuben slips out the door.

It's as if the provost had already forgotten Reuben was here. I'm not surprised; despite his size Reuben makes less noise than a cat, especially on these carpets. Is he one of the kids that have been at Saint Amos for so long he's just another gear in the machine?

"Well, it's still early days, of course, but I really do think teaching is something I'd like to do."

Gabriel takes a sip of his wine. Where my plate is practically splitting under the weight of all the food he piled on it, there's oceans of white china between his servings. I've never seen a chicken breast look so lonely before.

"You should attempt a full class during summer break."

I almost drop my fork. "Yeah. I'll look into that." I gulp at my soda and try to think of something to change the subject again.

My only intention is to score brownie points. But if I'm not careful, I'll have agreed to run a summer class for half the school before dinner is over.

"Does the school host anything fun during summer break?" I ask before shoving a fork full of food into my mouth.

Gabriel shakes his head, and then frowns up at me. He tuts quietly. "That's right. I must have forgotten to mention it. Saint Amos is closing over summer break. First time in almost five years, actually."

Closing?

Closing!

"Closing how?" I sit back in my seat. He wasn't wrong about my appetite—it comes and goes with my mood. I never eat when I'm uneasy, and for some reason his announcement fills me with dread.

"The students are leaving." Gabriel chews on a piece of chicken for a moment, looking thoughtful. He washes it down with a sip of wine and then puts down his cutlery. "We have extensive maintenance work to undertake. Several sections of the building will be cordoned off. It's just safer to send the students away until we reopen in the fall."

I put my cutlery down too. "Where are they going?"

"Some of our students are going home, or visiting extended family. The rest will be boarding at Sisters of Mercy in Devon."

Those that don't have homes.

"Like me?"

He nods. "Maybe you'll like it so much you decide to stay."

I swallow down more soda, but my mouth is still dry.

I've been codependent my entire life. I didn't have a choice, really. Not with parents who refused to send me to a regular school. The thought of what Father Gabriel's telling me sets my heart to racing.

"But I can stay here if I want?"

"Not during the break, but if you decide to return with the other students…" he spreads his hands, that absent smile of his not shifting one iota.

Then he pushes away his plate in favor of nursing his glass of wine. He takes a few sips as I try to get back into my meal, but it's impossible with him watching.

After a minute or so, he stands and goes over to the fireplace. He keeps his back to me as he lights a cigarette and takes a long drag.

"I'm not pushing you away, Trinity." He turns, smoke jettisoning from his nose. "I just want you to be happy. You're not happy here."

I hastily swallow. "But I am, Father. Really, I am."

"Don't lie to me, child." He puts his head to the side, his smile turning hard. "I know it can't be easy, a girl—*woman*—like you—" he points at me with the hand holding his cigarette "—surrounded by men."

What the hell am I supposed to say to that? It feels like a trap, like he wants me to admit I can't make it. That I want him to treat me like the friend I thought I was. That I need him to make an exception for the poor little girl who just lost her parents.

"I know these boys too well." He runs his fingers through his hair, takes another drag. His exhale obscures the fire for a moment. "So many troubled youths beneath this roof, Trinity. It would turn your hair white to hear their stories." He reaches out and flicks his cigarette ash into the ashtray.

"I know it won't be easy," I say as I slowly get to my feet. I hesitate, and then join him by the fire. "But…"

Lord, why is this so difficult to say?

"You're all I have left."

He glances at me for a second before his eyes go back to the fire. "You know that's not true, Trinity."

My chest fills with molten lava.

This again?

Really?

My hands are in fists, but it seems there's no way I can possibly unfurl them. If my feet weren't rooted to the spot, I'd storm out of here.

Why the fuck did I even come?

He *always* does this. He turns things around and makes it seem like it's your fault. That it's always been your fault, and you were too stupid and too egotistical and too—

vain

—to realize it.

"You know what?" I whirl to face him. My dress feels like a cheese grater against the inside of my wrists. "I *should* go to Sisters of Mercy. In fact, why don't I just go there right now since it's obvious you don't want me here."

I don't wait for his reply. My dress scrapes against my legs as I charge for the door leading out of this hell hole.

It's not just his cigarette smoke giving me a headache. Tears are waiting to fall.

Father Gabriel can say what he wants, I'm not biting.

My parents *believed.*

In God.

In the church.

In Father Gabriel.

Their lives—and subsequently, mine—were formed around the concept God is love. They say he notices when a damn swallow falls, but he couldn't be bothered to save two cherished members of his flock?

I don't give a fuck about me—God and me, we've never really been on speaking terms—but my parents deserved better than having their brains smeared over the tarmac because they hit a patch of ice.

I jerk at the door handle, but somehow Gabriel locked it when I wasn't looking because it won't open.

A hand appears, grasps mine, draws my fingers away.

I snatch it back. "Let go," I snap.

I try the door again. Gabriel slings a hand around my waist and drags me back.

"Let me go!" I shriek.

He lifts me bodily, and I start kicking and screaming like I'm possessed.

I'm vaguely aware Gabriel's trying to get me to calm down, but I can't stop fighting him.

I won't.

I'm a bottle of soda someone's been shaking and shaking and shaking.

Gabriel's just popped open the tab.

"I can't let you go," comes Gabriel's voice as I pause to draw breath. "Our holy Father won't allow it, child."

"Fuck you!" I beat at him with my fists, and he finally releases me when I land a blow to his midsection. "Fuck you, and fuck your God!" I stagger, stab a finger toward him. "You weren't there. He wasn't there. Never. Not once!"

Gabriel rushes forward, and I try to block him. But he's obviously had practice at calming down hysterical members of his clergy. He sidesteps easily before wrapping me in his arms and squeezing the life out of me.

My legs become weak and rubbery. Soon, they can no longer hold my weight.

We sink to the carpet. My ragged sobs and Gabriel's heavy breathing as he resists my struggles are the only sound for a moment. This close, he smells of red wine and cigarettes and a woody cologne.

There's a crash.

I hiccup in fright and turn to the door.

Reuben's standing there, shoulders bunched and hands held in blades. There's a look of such avid determination in his black eyes that I shrink away.

Inadvertently seeking comfort in Gabriel's arms.

"I heard…" Reuben cuts off.

"Everything is under control," the provost says.

Bitter words line up on my tongue, but I can't say anything with these hitching lungs of mine.

"Please, child." Gabriel's voice is tight, but calm. "Just take the dishes and leave. This does not concern you."

There's a clatter of crockery and cutlery as Reuben cleans the apartment.

Gabriel and I are still on the floor, and the fact has a wave of shame rolling through me. I turn and burrow my head against Gabriel's chest, and let a month's worth of anger, and hurt, and fear pour out of me.

So what if Reuben sees?

So what if the whole world knows how weak and pathetic I am?

It doesn't matter.

Because *I* don't matter.

If I did, then I'd still have my parents. I'd still be happy.

But I don't matter to anyone anymore.

Not even God.

15
ZAC

I sit up in bed and stare at the shadow of the man who's just stepped into my room.

"What are you doing here?" I ask.

Rube doesn't reply immediately. Instead, he moves about my room, hunting in the dark. Seconds later, a match flares and he lights the single candle on my desk.

My apartment is one of the smaller ones on the fourth floor of the east wing.

Reuben shouldn't be in this wing. He has a single student room on the west.

Light takes its time to seep into the shadows. Reuben sits on the corner of my bed, his profile cast in stark relief by the candle.

I don't need much more than a desk and a bed, so that's all there is this room. I'm fortunate enough to have an en-suite bathroom, but it's nothing more than a toilet and a shower.

"She was with him tonight."

There's no question who he's talking about.

Cass calls him Old Scratch, or Lucifer when he's feeling snarky. Reuben never addresses him by name, except if he's speaking to someone outside of our group. Then he uses the provost's full honorifics.

Apollo's terms of endearment are multitudinous. I think he commits several hours a week to thinking up new ones, in fact.

We're all obsessed with the past. We all suffer the same sick compulsion—to exact our revenge. We all pretend we have some form of control over ourselves.

Over each other.

"He fucked her?"

Rube snorts. "Dinner. And then confession."

"Confession?"

"He knows her parents. She said he's all she's got left."

My bed creaks as Reuben rocks forward, then back. Forward, then back.

"He kept touching her."

Shit.

That's why he came busting in here when he knows better than to expose our relationship like this. What he saw must have seriously unhinged him.

"Tell me."

Rube puts his head in his hands. "Holding her like she was his motherfucking child," he whispers.

I slide my hands under the blankets. At night, when the temperature drops, the pain in my ankles worsens. I draw my legs into a cross-legged seat and rub at the tendons, willing away their wretched ache.

"And she let him, Zac." Rube's whisper gains strength. "She let him put his sick, filthy hands on her like it meant nothing."

Christ, now my wrists are starting to ache too.

I need to cut this short. Rube's intensity gets to me sometimes. Makes it hard to stay focused. And I need to stay focused. My brothers depend on my stability. If it weren't for me, they'd still be scattered to the winds.

I brought us back together.

I forged their white-hot hatred into malleable steel.

I'll be the one to lead the charge on that fateful day. The one Cassius accused me of wanting to postpone.

Nothing could be further from the truth.

But I know what life is like. It's when you think you have everything under control that it all implodes.

F*or the Lord watches over the path of the godly, but the path of the wicked leads to destruction.*

"W e have to get rid of her," Rube mutters sullenly. "Let's do it tonight. Me and you. I know what room she's in —I checked."

Fuck. I surge forward, going onto my knees on the bed, and grab hold of Rube's shoulder. "Listen to me."

His muscles turn to stone under my hand.

"Reuben, listen to me."

Eventually, he turns to face me. Slowly, reluctantly, but he turns.

"We can't kill her."

"Yes we can," he states in a dead monotone. "It'll be easy."

"It'll draw attention to us."

"But she'll be gone."

"Rube. You're not listening."

"Better she's gone than she's with him."

Jesus, I'm losing him.

I get up and go to stand in front of him. He tilts back his head. I'm casting deep shadows over his face. "We don't know all the facts, Reuben. Remember the facts. They're important. More important than feelings." I press my hand to his chest. His flesh beneath his shirt is surprisingly warm, despite his cold heart.

"She doesn't know what he's going to do," Rube says. "Better she's gone, before she finds out."

I let out a sigh, and sink down in front of him. "We'll get rid of her, but without exposing ourselves. Without risking everything. Isn't that better?"

Rube's *humph* sounds doubtful. I need to call in reinforcements. We can't risk Reuben going rogue.

"Let's meet with the guys. We'll figure this out together."

When he doesn't respond, I grab his wrists and start massaging them. A second later, he catches hold of me and does the same. I grimace in pain before I can control my features. His hands are strong, and he knows exactly where it hurts.

"What's to figure out?" Rube says. "If we can't kill her, then we'll make her life unbearable. She won't have a choice. She'll have to leave."

His black eyes catch the light as he finally makes eyes contact with me again. If anyone saw him right now, they'd be convinced he was possessed by the Devil.

They'd piss themselves if they knew how right they were.

"No one comes to Saint Amos out of choice, Rube."

He studies me for a moment before his lips turn up into a cold smile.

"We did."

16

TRINITY

"What's wrong with you?"

I don't bother answering Jasper, just like I didn't bother getting undressed for bed last night, or showering, or even washing my face.

What's the point anyway?

"Hey, are you sick or something?"

"Sure," I mumble back. "Let's go with that."

Jasper mutters something under his breath before stomping out of the room. Thankfully, he closes the door behind him—I don't know if I have the energy to go after him and close it.

Minutes later, the prayer bell sounds.

I don't regret anything I said last night. I should…but I don't.

I can't remember how long I spent in Father Gabriel's room, in his arms. I know at some stage he lit a cigarette. That smell drove me out of myself just long enough to get to my feet and finally make it out of his room.

I walked the halls for a while. Half lost and panicking, half not giving a fuck if I ever found my way again.

But I eventually arrived back here in this little cubbyhole of a room. I climbed onto my bed, rolled myself in my blankets, and fell into a dreamless sleep.

That was a century ago. Or mere minutes.

Time is something that happens to other people.

The bedroom door opens, thumping against the wall.

I don't even flinch.

"You're sick?" Sister Miriam says from the doorway.

I consider the consequences of being as rude to her as I was to Jasper.

Not worth it.

"Yes," I mumble.

"Do you have a fever?"

"Yes."

Shoes clomp over the tiles. An icy hand clamps over my forehead. This time I do flinch, and I even manage to scramble up and move away from that hand.

Sister Miriam studies me for a moment. "You've been crying."

No fucking duh. Did my swollen eyes give it away?

"Come. Get up."

I shake my head. "Please, I'll go to class. I just…I just need to sleep for a little longer."

"You *will* get up *now*. You *will* wash. You *will* eat breakfast with the others."

I wish I could spontaneously burst into tears right now. I'm not sure if it would help, but I've got to believe even someone as cold-hearted as Sister Miriam might be moved by the sight of tears.

Fuck, who am I kidding? Anyone who works in a place like this has got to be immune to shit like that by now.

I'm sure that's the only way people stay sane around here.

I obviously took too long to answer her. Her mouth twisting

into a sour grimace, Miriam darts forward, catches hold of the shoulder of my dress, and drags me out of bed.

"That wasn't a request, Miss Malone."

Miss Malone.

She hauls open my closet and takes down one of the hangers. The next moment, I'm clutching a brown dress to my chest.

It's not as thick as the one I'm wearing. This is normal fabric. Still stiff, but in a way that suggests it hasn't been through the wash enough times to be soft.

A new dress, made just for me.

It should make me happy, even superficially, but instead all I can think about is how ashamed I was last night. Sitting there in a heap on Gabriel's floor.

Did Reuben tell anyone?

Does someone like him even have friends to gossip with?

Miriam draws back the sleeve of her habit to check a dainty wristwatch. On her, it looks like the string on a roll of salami.

"You have half an hour. Plenty of time to wash up and get down to breakfast." Her eyes narrow. "I'll know if you don't show. I'll know if you don't eat. Don't test me, Miss Malone. You'll regret it."

I scowl after her as she leaves. I believe her—after all, she knew I was playing sick.

Jasper.

He must have said something to her.

I'm going to *kill* him.

Fuck his grades. I don't care if he fails. In fact, I hope he has to repeat the entire year. Maybe then he'll think twice about snitching on someone.

I head for the showers, but I don't make it all the way. A few yards from the door, I can already hear the commotion inside. I don't know how many boys are in there, but even one would have been too many. Is night the only time I stand a chance to shower alone?

This is such bullshit.

I go back to my room and flop down on my bed. When the bell rings for breakfast, I lay there for a few seconds before my brain wills my body into action.

Self-preservation in action.

I drag off my old dress and slip into the new one. I *really* need a shower, but I'll wait until tonight. In the meantime, the smell of washing powder on this dress smells will have to do.

The fabric is baggy around my boobs and too tight around my hips. It's so uncomfortable that I stand for a good minute seriously considering wearing the old, scratchy dress. At least it was baggy all over.

When I get down to the dining hall, everyone's already seated. Sister Miriam is stalking down the aisles, head poking forward like she's making sure no one's thinking dirty thoughts.

Or is she looking for me?

I hurry over to the tray table and grab the lone tray sitting there. As soon as I turn around, I spot Jasper.

Because he was watching me with a concerned look on his face.

Holy crap, was I *that* rude to him? Or does he know I got into a heap of trouble with Miriam? That latter seems more likely, especially since he moves aside and beckons me over with a flick of his wrist.

"Thanks," I mumble as I slide onto the bench beside him.

He studies me for a moment and then shrugs. "Nice dress."

"Fuck off."

His eyebrows go to his hairline, but he doesn't reply. Perry's sitting opposite us on the bench, but he doesn't even look up from his tray.

I hear Sister Miriam approach from the other side of the room.

Clomp, clomp.

Grimacing faintly, I peel the plastic wrap off the tray. "Ew," I murmur, using my spoon to poke at the beige gruel slopped in my tray.

Normally, there's something different in each of the little hollows—a piece of toast, scrambled eggs, oatmeal.

Not today.

Today it's all oatmeal. And it looks gross enough to be from last week's batch.

"Running low on donations or something?" I mutter, glancing over at Jasper's plate.

My spoon sags.

Jasper's tray is full of the usual—in fact, it looks like he even got a fucking breakfast sausage.

What the hell?

"Maybe they ran out?" Jasper whispers.

Clomp, clomp.

I heap some of the disgusting oatmeal onto my spoon and toy with it for effect as Miriam comes up behind me. There's a tug on the back of my dress, and suddenly my boobs fill the bodice.

"We'll need to take more measurements," Miriam says, as if I'm not surrounded by a table full of boys. "Come see me this afternoon."

I'm blushing so hard I don't even hear her walking away.

"Here," Jasper says.

I glance at him. He's holding out his sausage on the end of his fork.

When I look up at him, he drops his eyes.

"Not hungry," I say, pushing away my plate.

I stand and go over to the far side of the room, ignoring the eyes surreptitiously following me. I pour myself a cup of coffee, hesitate, and then double the amount of sugar I normally do.

I'm sure I'm going to need the energy today.

On the way back to my seat, I spot movement across the room.

Of course.

My day wouldn't be complete without someone filming me for no apparent reason. It's blatantly obvious he's got the lens focused on me—it tracks me as I cross the room.

I thump down into my seat and point at him, leaning sideways to Jasper. I keep my voice low even though Sister Miriam left the hall minutes ago.

"Who is that?"

Jasper frowns as he looks up. "Think his name's Apollo."

Perry turns in his seat and comes back with a nod. "Yeah. That's Apollo. Why?"

"Because I'm sick of him filming me." I stand and dust my hands. "And I'm sure Sister Miriam won't like it when I tell her what he's been doing."

"You're gonna tell?" Jasper frowns up at me.

I put my hands on my waist and glare down at him. "*You're* lecturing me about snitching?"

The hall goes silent.

My cheeks instantly turn red.

But I hold my ground, even when Jasper frowns in confusion. "I didn't say anything. Father Gabriel asked us where you were before he started prayers this morning." Jasper throws out a hand to encompass every student in the school.

Even Apollo and his damned video camera.

"He asked the whole school, and when no one said they'd seen you, then he asked me specifically." Jasper snorts and leans back, scooping up a heap of scrambled eggs with his fork. "I ain't gonna lie for you."

I deflate a little at that. I guess I should have realized Jasper wouldn't snitch, but I hadn't thought Gabriel would ask after me either.

I sink back into my seat and mutter out a low, "Sorry."

"Yeah, well, fuck you," Jasper says. He stabs his fork toward me again. "Now eat the fucking sausage."

I stare at the oily sausage, and then up at him.

You know what? Thank *fuck* my tray was the last one and all I got was prison gruel. I'm glad I couldn't go shower this morning because the place was infested with boys.

We've been through this little dance, the Universe and I. It seems to forget that even if it knocks me down, I'll pop right back up again. A little like punching fog, and a lot like punching a balloon.

I slide the sausage off his fork and bite carefully into it. It's not great, but anything's better than the gruel.

"And if you don't want to eat crap, get here sooner," he mutters.

"Yes, Mom."

My skin goes cold when I hear what I said, but it gets a chuckle from Jasper and a snicker from Perry, and I don't want to ruin that.

How long will it take before a single phrase like that doesn't stab icicles through my heart?

Another month? A year?

Maybe never.

However long it'll take I can handle.

Because, honestly…how much worse can this possibly get?

17

TRINITY

Despite its awful start, my day seems to take a good turn. I made progress with Jasper today. Heck, we might even be able to get along after all.

I'm still buzzing on that high when I get to my first class. English—taught by the very severe and very dry Sister Sharon. I never knew someone who could suck the fun out of literature as much as she could. But I'm determined to get through the lesson with a smile on my face.

Until I see who's sitting in my chair.

"Cassius, please return to your usual seat," Sharon says.

I'm pretty sure I would have remembered if the handsome sociopath of a hallway monitor was in my class.

Nope. Definitely a first.

"I don't think she'll be able to see over my head," Cassius says. He sounds one-hundred percent genuine in his concern, but there's a gleam in his eyes that makes me wonder what the hell he's up to.

Surely he should have graduated last year already? He looks at least a year too old to be in my grade.

I stand at the front of the class, gripping my books like a lifeline as I wait for the situation to resolve itself.

"I suppose you're right," Sister Sharon says. She turns to me and then points to the seat in front of Cassius. "Take a seat Trinity. You're holding up the class."

Me?

I narrow my eyes at Cassius, and in response he slides an inch lower in his seat, props his elbow on the table, and leers at me like I'm a pork chop he's been salivating over since his last meal. Feeling overly exposed in my ill-fitting dress, never mind every eye in the class watching me again, I make my way to the seat in front of Cassius and sit down.

Try to sit down.

At the last moment, there's a flash of movement under Cassius's desk. The chair isn't there anymore.

Of course Sister Sharon had turned her back on the class to write something on the board.

Of course I lose my balance and land on my ass with a very comedic 'oomph' while my books and notepad go flying.

Of course everyone starts laughing.

And, of fucking *course*, Sister Sharon looks back as Cassius rushes over to help me up.

"Quiet!" Sharon whacks the edge of her desk with her wooden ruler. Then she turns shrewd eyes on me. "When you're ready, Trinity, I'd like to start class?"

The fall must have knocked out my senses, because I don't even struggle when Cassius kindly grasps my elbow and helps me to my feet. Or when he slides the chair under my ass like he's seating me for a dinner date.

"New Girl's a bit of a klutz," he says, loud enough that everyone can hear.

I glare at him.

His fingertips trail along the back of my neck as he moves around his desk and takes his seat.

I sit stiff and unmoving for the first half of the lesson, afraid that even the slightest movement will bring undue attention to myself while hoping that sitting still will make the back of my neck stop tingling.

I don't succeed at either.

"Turn to page eighty-four of your textbooks."

I glance around and spot my English textbook laying on its back beside me on the floor. Thank the Lord Sharon didn't see it there. She hands out knuckle raps if you dare to dog-end a single page in your textbook. Imagine what she'd do if she saw—

As soon as the book is in my hands, I know something's wrong.

A spike of dread shoots through me when I turn it over.

What the hell?

This isn't my textbook. Mine was a grubby second-hand copy —this one's squeaky new.

I risk a quick glance over my shoulder.

Cassius is slouched in his seat, his long legs stretched out in front of him, ankles crossed. He has a textbook propped up on the desk in front of him.

That's my textbook.

"Trinity?"

I spin back to face Sister Sharon. I open my mouth to apologize right off the bat for whatever she wants to charge me with, but then her eyes move down and land on the textbook.

"Have you forgotten how books work?" she asks sweetly, and my stomach sinks like a rock dropped down a well.

"No, Sister."

"Then open it."

Something tells me that's not a good idea.

I should tell her it's not my book, that Cassius switched it, but it's obvious he's one of her favored students. Plus, I never got around to writing my name in the front.

Screw it. I'm not gonna let this guy ruffle my feathers. My ass is still aching from my fall—I think I bruised it—and I don't want him to think any of this shit affects me.

WWJD, right? He'd turn the other fucking cheek.

But I can't move. I'm terrified.

Sharon's eyes narrow to slits. She walks over and uses the tip of her ruler to flip open the cover.

I stare down at a photo-realistic drawing of Brother Zachary. Then I tip my head up and gape at Sister Sharon as my cheeks catch fire.

Why?

Why would Cassius do this to me?

"Wow," comes a breathy whisper from behind. "That's downright blasphemous, little slut."

"I didn't draw that!" I scoot back my chair and jump up. "Sister, I swear this isn't my textbook."

Thwack!

Everyone in class except Cassius flinches when her wooden ruler slaps down on the book. Sister Sharon has good aim—she manages to cover Zachary's penciled ass and the cock he's got shoved in my ass.

"I could come up with better excuses in my sleep," Sister Sharon says, her wrinkled lips pursing with disgust.

I half-turn to glance at Cassius.

He's sitting there with his elbows propped on the table, his head in his hands, mouth open with shock like he doesn't know exactly where this book came from.

"Sit!"

My ass thumps into the chair.

"Hand out. Flat on the desk."

I turn wide, pleading eyes to Sister Sharon but my hand's

already moving over the wooden desk. She uses the tip of her rule to flip closed the textbook, and then taps the far side of my desk.

"Here."

My hand slides to the spot she selected. I close my eyes and drop my head, stifling a gasp when she brings her ruler down on the back of my hand.

Thwack.

Thwack.

Thwack!

It's like she's trying to beat the sexual deviancy out of me. I keep my head down even when I hear her walking away. Then I glance back at Cassius without lifting it.

There's no mistaking the satisfied gleam in his eyes.

"Why?" I mouth to him, blinking back tears of pain. I slide my hand back and cradle it in my lap as I wait for his answer.

"Eyes up front!" Sharon slaps her ruler on the edge of her desk, and the whole class sits up, me included.

When she turns her back again, I'm already anticipating the warm breath on the side of my neck, and Cassius's smooth voice in my ears.

"I don't like you, New Girl," Cassius murmurs. "I think you should go back to where you came from."

"Fuck you." I sit forward so I don't have to listen to him anymore.

A hand knots in my curly hair. Cassius wrenches my head back. I'm so shocked, I don't even gasp.

His lips brush the shell of my ear as he whispers. "I'm just getting started. If I were you, I'd find a new school."

I spend the rest of the lesson silently seething as I try to ignore my aching knuckles and scalp.

As soon as the bell rings Cassius swaggers past me and out the door.

I scoop up my things and hurry after him.

Words are going to be said. Possibly even yelled. I won't stand for this and Cassius is going to know it in the next five seconds.

"Not so fast, Trinity."

I skid to a halt by Sister Sharon's desk.

"Sister?" I do my best to look humbled and not like I'm on my way to attack someone in the hallway.

She perches on the edge of her chair before taking a piece of paper from her drawer. Bowing her head, she starts writing. "This behavior is unacceptable."

I open my mouth but she doesn't allow me to speak.

"You've caused enough disruption by joining my class so late in the year—I won't stand for further theatrics."

I'm being outright bullied and she thinks I'm trying to get attention?

"When is your next lesson with Brother Zachary?"

A cold dread seeps into my bones. "Why?"

"I ask the questions," Sharon says. Her pen scratches on the paper as she signs whatever she was writing with a violent flourish.

"Right now."

"Good. You will take this letter—" she looks up and folds up the piece of paper she was writing on "—and you will hand it to Brother Zachary the moment you set foot in his class."

She holds out the paper. It's not even in an envelope. But as if she can read my mind, she adds, "It's for his eyes only."

This can't be good.

My fingers are numb when I take the paper from her. I turn and head for the door.

"And Trinity?"

I pause, biting the inside of my lip.

"If you disrupt my class again, there will be severe consequences."

My heart's still pounding in my throat when I make my way down the hall.

Instead of confronting Cassius about his prank, I slink down the hall and pray no one notices me. I clomp down the stairs and stand in front of Zachary's classroom door.

A student hurries toward me from the other side of the hall, and for a moment I'm convinced he's a messenger about to make my day even worse.

Instead, he pauses about a yard away from the door and watches me intently. "You going in, or what?"

Shit, I didn't even recognize him. It's Simon—a kid from my psych class. I step back and let him go ahead of me while I try and gather my courage.

But it's a lost cause—I'm rattled.

There's no denying I have a target on my back. But who put it there?

And *why?*

Zachary looks up from his desk and then down at the paper I'm holding out. It trembles ever so slightly. He takes it from me, the class falling silent behind me when he opens it. Two of the students from my English class are also in psych, but I'm positive the rest of the class already knows about what happened in English.

Did any of them see the drawing?

I'd almost peeked at the letter when I was standing outside, but then I thought back to that stained glass window I'd seen on my first tour through Saint Amos.

That big eye in the sky.

Always watching.

Omnipotent.

Anyway, I don't want to know what it says.

Ignorance is bliss, right?

Zachary folds open the letter and scans it. He closes it up and slips it into his desk drawer. Then his eyes fall to the textbook I'm crushing against my chest.

I'd forgotten all about it, but as soon as his eyes settle on the hardback cover, the drawing inside flashes through my mind like a still from a porno film.

I imagine, anyway. I've never seen one. I've never had access to the Internet without parental supervision. The dirtiest book in the library I was allowed to use was Pride and Prejudice.

"The book," Zachary says evenly, when I don't make a move.

I hand it over reluctantly as my cheeks grow hot.

Zachary flips open the front cover and goes to turn the page. His hand freezes and then drops to the bottom of the page.

"Surprisingly accurate," he murmurs just loud enough for me to hear.

My ears start to buzz. "What?"

He flips the cover closed and sits back in his seat. Slowly shaking his head, Zachary studies me with magnetic eyes. "What are we going to do with you, Miss Malone?"

"It's not my book," I say.

He cocks his head. "You stole this from someone?"

"What? No!"

"Then how did you come to be in possession of it?" His eyes narrow with irritation.

The name is on the tip of my tongue, but I can't say it. Which is ridiculous—if Zachary and Sister Sharon knew what Cassius had done, he'd be the one facing off with Zachary right now.

He'd be the one about to be punished.

He'd...

No, nothing would happen to him. It's obvious Sister Sharon has a soft spot for him, and I'm pretty sure I saw him visiting Zachary on my first day here. It was only a glimpse as we passed in the hallway, but I'd recognize those blue eyes anywhere.

I could try and accuse him, but I was the outsider.

The outcast.

No one was going to believe anything I said. It burns like righteous fire inside me, the fact that telling the truth would only get me into more trouble, but I'm not stupid enough to believe I'm capable of convincing these strangers.

Maybe I'll go talk to Gabriel. If anyone would believe me, he would.

So I drop my gaze and hang my head like I'm overwhelmed with remorse.

"Take your seat," Zachary says.

When I reach for the textbook, he lays a hand on it to stop me. "We'll discuss this after class."

In a weird, hallucinogenic moment, I think he's talking about the drawing. What was there to discuss? The drawn-on expression of ragged bliss on my face as he pounds me from behind? The fact that I'm bent over this very desk?

Or how the longer I think about the drawing, the more I can't stop thinking about what it would feel like, being with him.

I don't think I'm going to make it to the end of class.

God damn it, it had been almost impossible to keep a straight face when I'd seen what Cassius had drawn inside that English textbook.

I hadn't wanted to risk a face-to-face meeting this soon after our last one, so I'd sent out a group text to my brothers early this morning. I hadn't mentioned much about what Rube had said, just that our goal today was to make Trinity's life pure hell.

I should have known Apollo and Cass would take it as a challenge.

I'd left the details up to them and, looking back, that might not have been the best decision. I've already caught a few whispered rumors about something happening at breakfast with Trinity. And I know she was absent from prayers this morning, although I'm not sure if my brothers had anything to do with that or not.

I'll get their full reports later this afternoon.

At least I made sure to tell Reuben not to go anywhere near her. I don't trust him in his current state of mind. This close, with so much at stake? It would be too easy for him to unravel.

I throw myself into my lesson like I always do, but I'm distracted.

Cassius's drawing is to blame.

Her shapely thighs and plump ass. Curls bouncing around her naked shoulders.

In the drawing, I have both hands on her hips, leaving her perky little tits free to bob.

I'd had every intention of holding her back after class and putting the fear of God into her…but that picture had roused something that had lain dormant inside me for a long, long time.

Maybe it was her innocence. From the way she keeps blushing, or how she's always hiding behind her books to shield her body from inquisitive eyes, it's obvious she's inexperienced.

Shy, and secretive, and naive.

But with just enough backbone that, for a moment, I'd thought she would rat out Cassius. But then she'd chickened out and had taken the blame like a good little soldier.

I need a clear head right now. I can't afford to be distracted by what I think her ass would look like while I fucked her from behind.

Those types of thoughts are what lead to acts of deviance and perversion in the first place. This is more natural than the ones I'm normally obsessed with, but regardless.

She looks relieved when I don't say anything as she passes my table after the bell rings at the end my lesson. And when she glances back over her shoulder, her frown makes me wonder if I'm being too soft.

That, or she's wondering about my response to the letter.

I thought I'd been casual as fuck, staring down at that drawing, but maybe I hadn't.

I'd hoped to join the boys in their fun, but I can't be as close to this as I'd wanted.

One of us has to keep a level head.

19

TRINITY

I'm famished by the time lunch comes around. I head for the dining hall as quickly as I can. While the day had been sunny for the most part, gray-bottomed clouds are scooting in from the horizon. Every time one of them passes over the sun, the temperature drops a few degrees.

The fact that the smell of stew makes my mouth water is a testament to how hungry I am. There are about thirty students in the hall when I arrive, most seated with their trays in front of them.

I hurry over to the tray table, already reaching for one of the covered trays when something catches my eye.

A bright pink post-it has been attached to one of the trays nearest the edge of the table.

TRINITY MALONE

The tray is isolated by now—obviously no one dared touch it.

I pick it up and grimace.

More gruel.

Gray. Pasty. Disgusting.

The other trays are heaped with vegetable stew and fat slices of chunky bread spread thick with butter.

This. Is. *Such*. Bullshit.

I take my tray and make a beeline for the kitchen. I hurry up to the first cook I spot and thrust out the tray with its blatantly pink sticker. "What is this?"

The cook—a guy that could have been my age or a year younger—gives me a condescending scan before sneering at me. "Your food," he says.

"Why don't I get stew?"

"Because we don't make special food around here."

I frown at him. "Special? What are you talking about?"

He dismisses me with a flick of his hand and then pushes me aside with his shoulder. I start after him before someone calls out a few yards behind me. "Orders from the top."

I turn to another cook. "I don't understand." I put the tray down on a nearby stainless steel workbench. "I don't eat anything special. I just want normal food like everyone else."

"Well, we got told you're vegan and have these—" the guy shrugs, working his shoulders for a second "—lactose-gluten-sodium allergies and shit." He points at the tray. "That's pretty much all we got that you can eat."

"But…I'm not."

He shrugs and turns back to peeling potatoes.

"Can't I—is there any normal food left? Even just some bread?"

"Not for you. Not unless our orders change."

"Okay, so who?" I storm up to him, stabbing a finger at the floor. "Tell me who gave the order."

Another shrug. "Ask Apollo. He's the one who came and told us."

Apollo?

The guy with the video camera?

What. The. Actual. Fuck?

It couldn't be a coincidence.

What if Sister Miriam's the one who told me to film you in the first place?

But that doesn't make any sense. None at all. Sister Miriam can pretty much watch me all the time. More so than Apollo can, if she wanted. I mean, she literally stripped me down in the laundry room to take my measurements.

Another prank then? I'd thought breakfast was my own bad luck, but maybe someone had taken off the post-it at the last minute, seeing it was the only tray left uncollected.

Or maybe he wanted to make *sure* I got another serving of gruel.

Why?

Why the hell was I being targeted like this?

My mind scrambles as I head back to the dining hall, leaving my disgusting lunch behind. I'm starving, but I'd rather pass out from hunger than be subjected to a prank like this.

I meet Apollo as he's coming back inside the kitchen. He's wheeling a much smaller trolley than the one he uses for the students. There's still one wide, covered tray on it that looks similar to the one Reuben brought to Father Gabriel's room the other night.

"Hey!"

He's walking backward, dragging the trolley after him as he pushes open the door with his back. He smirks at me over his shoulder. "How ya doing, pretty thing?"

"Who told you I couldn't eat normal food?"

His smirk turns into a grin. "I don't kiss and tell."

"I knew it," I say, stabbing a finger at him as I pass. "You made it up."

"You gonna tell on me?" he calls.

My hand is on the door, but I don't push it open. I stand

there for a second, listening to the sound of the trolley wheels squeaking. Then a pair of sneakers coming closer.

Apollo comes into view from the corner of my eye. He leans against the wall near the hinge of the door and crosses his arms over his chest.

"Because you can go rat me out if you want, but it won't change anything."

"I'll get to eat proper food again," I snap.

"Maybe. Maybe not." He sighs and leans his head against the wall too, scratching at his forehead with his thumbnail. There's a mark there, under the hair hanging in his eyes. A star-shaped scar. An old sports injury maybe?

"Wouldn't it just be easier to leave? I mean, this place sucks ass. Why the fuck would you want to come to school here anyway?"

I gape at him. "What the hell does it matter to you where I go to school?" I take a step closer and poke a finger in his chest. "I don't need your permission to be here."

His smile becomes a grin. "You're cute when you're mad."

"Fuck you!" I blurt out. "You'd better stop—"

My only warning is the sudden stutter of his eyes as he catches sight of something behind me. I spin around, already clamping my mouth closed.

Too late.

I'd been so caught up with yelling at Apollo I hadn't spotted Sister Miriam coming into the kitchen.

"Sister, he—" I point behind me, and even turn a little to make it clear who I'm accusing.

Don't ever turn your back on an angry nun.

She grabs my ear and yanks so hard I swear it almost comes off. I yell and shoot to my tiptoes so my ear doesn't tear free.

"Enough," Miriam snaps. "Enough, enough, *enough*!" The last word booms through the kitchen like a bomb going off.

Where there'd been the idle clatter of pans and cutlery, everything cuts off. The handful of people inside the kitchen are all staring at me.

Then Sister Miriam does the unthinkable.

She drags me out of the kitchen and through the dining hall...by my fucking ear.

Tears streak down my cheeks from the pain and humiliation, but I already know that whatever's coming next is going to be a thousand-fold worse.

This is what happens when you fight back, Trinity.

Should've eaten the goddamn gruel. But no. Suddenly, you think you deserve a slice of normal.

Wrong.

So very fucking wrong.

No one in this place is your friend. They'll never be your friend. Even Gabriel's already trying to get rid of you. Maybe you should pack your things and start walking.

The forest will be more hospitable than this place.

TRINITY

Thankfully, Miriam doesn't drag me all the way by my ear. A few yards outside the dining hall, close to the small prayer room, she releases me.

With a flick of her arm, she consults her little watch and then glares at me for a second. Her eyes move to the prayer room. She points. "You stay in there until I come for you."

When I don't move, she grabs me by my collar and drags me bodily through that little arched door. I stumble when she shoves me inside and catch my knee on one of the chairs. Whimpering, I turn as she starts closing the door in my face.

She pauses when there's little more than her face showing. "Best you pray to God that I've cooled down before I come back, else you won't have a strip of hide left."

She bangs the door in my face.

I cup my ear, massaging at my itchy, stretched skin where it meets my scalp with one hand and rubbing my knee where I bumped my leg with the other.

"Are you all right?"

No.

No, no, no, no, no!

Come on!

I spin on legs that feel like they've turned to rubber. A big shape unfolds from the small chancel and slowly turns to face me.

Reuben.

I swallow an angry sob and move back, fumbling behind me for the handle. After everything that's happened today, the only logical conclusion is that I'm about to die.

Terror traps a broken scream in my throat when I don't find the handle. When my fingertips brush blank wood. I don't dare look around, because then he'll pounce me and do God knows what to me.

Maybe bash my head on the floor till my skull cracks open.

Fuck, he could probably crush my head between his hands if he wanted.

"Please."

Wood.

Wood.

Brick.

"Don't."

Reuben ducks his head, and slowly replaces his rosary.

Brick.

Wood.

Brick.

Where the *fuck* is the door handle?

I have to risk it.

I glance around, all the while my skin crawling with invisible tarantulas.

He's still standing by the pulpit. He hasn't moved closer. My heart thumps in relief, but I don't stop looking for the handle.

"Let me show you," he says, and steps closer.

I let out a small squeal of panic and turn my back fully so I can find the damn handle.

But there's nothing there—just smooth wood.

I'm locked inside with a psycho.

My stomach plummets to hell.

"Where's the handle?" I yell, turning back to him. He's closer now, but not like the first time I saw him here. He's taking his time, edging forward as if he knows there's no rush.

"I can show you," he says calmly. "But only if you promise to calm down."

"Sure. I'm calm. See?" I sweep out my arms and then hug them to my chest. I step back as far as I can, practically disappearing into the corner of the small room as he reaches me.

"Why are you so scared of me?"

Because you're psychotic!

"I'm not. It's Miriam. I don't want to be here when she gets back."

"You'll get in trouble if you run away."

"I don't care!" I hastily lower my voice. "I mean, she knows where to find me. And I really have to pee. I'll get her outside."

"You haven't prayed yet."

Fuck. *Fuck!*

He's just standing there.

Liar. He won't open the door for me. It was just an excuse to get closer without me bolting. I glance to the side. I can make it over the chairs. Scramble to the front of the room. We'll chase each other around in circles until Miriam comes back.

But what if he catches me before she returns?

What will he do to me?

Fear of the unknown drives icy panic through me. I shiver once, hard, and then I can't seem to stop.

"Are you cold?"

"Please just open the door."

He shrugs. Then he pushes his hand against the wood, close to where the handle would be on the outside. The door sinks inward a little, and then bounces open a crack. There's a little rift where he slides in his fingers, and then he pulls it open.

I race for the opening, knowing I won't make it, but not willing to stand there and accept my fate.

Reuben presses the door closed in my face. I freeze, standing an inch away from the wood, too frightened to move.

His palm slides down the wood as he lets out a long breath through his nose. He moves closer until his clothes brush against mine.

Blood roars in my ears. It drives heat into my cheeks and constricts my lungs.

"You should pray."

"Okay," I manage breathlessly. "I'll pray."

"Ask God for forgiveness."

"I will." Forcing a swallow, I add, "I'll do it when I'm done with Miriam. Outside."

"You'll do it now. Inside."

This close, his smell is everywhere. Something floral, something rich, something woody. Masculine, but soft at the same time.

"Okay." I turn, assuming he'd step back so I head over to the pulpit.

Isn't this what you do when you're held hostage by a crazy person? You humor them, keep them talking until the cops come.

I have no idea where Sister Miriam went or how long she'll be away, but if I can keep up this pretense…

At first he doesn't move. With his hand on the door behind me, he's close to boxing me in. Admittedly, he's not the ogre I first thought him to be. He's tall and broad, but he's not a steroid-junkie.

I'd probably have thought him seriously attractive if I hadn't been so terrified of him.

Weird, how I've met so many handsome guys over the past few days. And in a place like Saint Amos? That's bordering on freaky.

"Here. This will help you focus your intent." Reuben lifts his rosary from around his neck and slips it over my head.

That's where the smell is coming from. His rosary is made from rose-wood. The sweet smell envelops me as soon as he slips the beads over my head. But there's something else mixed in there. His own scent. He must stroke the beads while he prays.

And I'm guessing he prays a lot.

My fear fades a little, even though I know it shouldn't. There's no guarantee that because he regularly prays to God that he won't hurt me.

But it makes it easier to believe he might have a conscience. Threatening me is one thing, but actually physically hurting me? That's crossing a line. One he might not be able to because of his beliefs.

I clutch that thought as I slip past him and stride over to the pulpit. It's only three yards away, so it's still like he's right behind me when I sink down onto the pillow laid in front of the chancel.

Resting on my knees, I put my palms on my thighs and duck forward. Hopefully I look like the real thing.

But as I'm kneeling there, the smell of Reuben's necklace getting stronger and stronger, his presence growing until it fills every inch of the room...I start feeling more and more like a phony.

I've never prayed. Not once.

Sure, I've recited the Father's Prayer. I've read the bible. I've sat in church more often than I can count.

But I've never prayed.

I never felt that connection my parents and Father Gabriel claimed to have.

I was always acting.

Reuben knows it.

The last thing I want to do is make him angry. Should I stand? Give him back his necklace?

Fabric rustles behind me.

He exhales somewhere close behind before sliding his hands onto my shoulders.

I risk a peek. He's kneeling behind me. "What are you doing?" I whisper.

Another breath. It warms the back of my neck where my hair's been scooped up into an attempt at a bun.

"I'm praying for you," he says in his sonorous voice.

"Why?"

"Because I'm guessing you don't know how. And trust me, you need all the help you can get."

Sister Miriam comes to fetch me sometime later. Reuben never lifted his hands, and he never said another word to me again. I'd slipped into a trance while energy moved between us.

I'm not being new age about it—I *felt* it. My entire body came alive at his touch. Every disastrous thing that happened up to that point had melted away.

I was at peace.

I felt loved.

I'm convinced he actually managed to contact God on my behalf.

That, or he's some kind of god himself.

When Miriam comes for me, I'm not frightened anymore. Not of him. Not of her.

Not of this place, or my future, or my past.

I'm ready to face whatever she has waiting.

She notices that when I leave the prayer room.

But it doesn't change anything.

I guess around here nothing ever changes. Rules are rules. I misbehaved and for that I have to be punished.

I just wish it wasn't her handing out my penance.

ZAC

"This isn't working is it?" Apollo says as soon as I get within earshot. "Why isn't it working, Zac?" He was pacing, thumbs hooked into his belt, but as soon as I'm in the crypt's sunken center, he sinks into a chair and starts jiggling his leg.

He's not the only agitated one. Reuben is perched on the edge of his seat, meaty hands clasped and dangling between his legs. Cassius is smoking a blunt, but with an intensity that belies his slouched body and deadpan expression.

"I don't know," I mutter. I snatch the blunt from Cass's fingertips just as he's about to take a drag, and give it a hefty tug. "But she's fucking testing my patience."

Apollo snorts.

Between the four of us, I'm the rock. It takes a shit load to piss me off or deter me. Weather-beaten, but still standing.

Because, long before the Brotherhood, there was only me.

Then came Apollo. Then came Reuben. Then came Cassius.

Even back then, we had no notion of revenge. For us it was all about survival. Every day was a silent victory.

Every hour.

Every fucking second.

This girl is getting under my skin. Anyone in her position would have been out that door in ten seconds flat.

"She's a fucking masochist, that's what she is," Cass says. "But you were right. She didn't say a word about me to anyone." He sits forward, imitating Reuben. "She didn't, right?"

"Not to me." I shake my head and take another drag. Then I have to smile, because it's fucking rare either of us gets the chance. "That drawing though…"

Cassius's face lights up with a grin. He leans across and taps Apollo's chest with the back of his hand. "Bro, you should have seen it."

Apollo looks up at me. "You still got it, right?"

I nod. "Some of Cass's best work." I study the blunt between my fingers. "She's stronger than we thought. Braver. We might have to change tactics."

I take a last hit of the joint. It's almost down to the filter, but I offer it to Rube like I always do. I'm already retracting my hand on automatic when he takes it from me.

Apollo's jiggling leg freezes. Cassius turns to stare.

Reuben studies the joint, and then eviscerates the last quarter-inch of weed. I almost dart forward and retrieve it before he inhales the fucking filter too.

He drops it to the floor and crushes it out under a massive shoe.

When he exhales, Cassius and Apollo disappear behind the smoke cloud.

"She's not brave, she's just stubborn," Reuben says. He shifts in his seat before glancing hesitantly in my direction.

"What do you mean?"

"I know you said I shouldn't go near her—"

I'm on my feet in a second. "What did you do?"

"Nothing." Reuben spreads his hands. "She came to me."

"What? Why?" Apollo demands.

"Doesn't matter," Rube tells Apollo before turning back to me. "I didn't do anything. I just…prayed with her."

"Rube…" My voice is dangerously low. "What did you say to her?"

He shakes his head. "Nothing. But I saw she was more scared of me than Sister Miriam."

"If she's so scared, then why hasn't she ratted us out?" Cass demands. "I mean, all she has to do—"

"Shame. Denial. Fear of the consequences. I could go on." I take my seat, sitting back and spreading my legs. This isn't comfort, but when the four of us are together it's like I've come home after a long day. These brief meetings in the crypt are our versions of Sunday lunch.

Out there, we're just a bunch of kids.

In here, we're motherfucking assassins.

Unfortunately, Trinity Malone only sees us as we are outside these walls.

"Textbook behavior," I add.

Every eyebrow twitches at this—even Reuben's.

"So what do we do? The girl's not budging," Apollo mutters, sitting back and crossing his arms over his chest.

"That's just it…" I swing my leg up, resting my ankle over my knee. "We've been treating her like a girl. Like a delicate piece of glass we don't dare break."

Cassius chuckles. "I can break her for—"

"Cass!"

His eyes flick up to mine. "What? She suddenly so fucking special or something?"

"That's a bit hypocritical, don't you think?" I ask, tilting my head. We've been down this path of reason before—Cassius always ends up in the fucking bushes.

"She's a slut anyway," Cassius says.

I don't even bother looking at him.

We've all got twisted world views. But we also have an excuse. We never got to see the world as other kids did. Our crayon drawings didn't have rainbows and stick-figure family portraits. Ours—if we'd ever had any—would have been black and red landscapes crosshatched with repressed pain.

Cassius thinks everyone's a closet slut, and would fuck anything that moves if I didn't reign him in.

Apollo is a full out voyeur. He'd rather film someone masturbating than actually have sex with them.

Reuben will probably die a virgin. Kind of.

Me? It's best if I became a priest and swore celibacy for the rest of my life. Because unlike my brothers, there's only one thing that actually brings me joy.

They'd crucify me in a heartbeat if they ever found out what it was.

"She'll break," I say, shifting in my seat.

Reuben's staring at me so hard it's like he's digging through my brain with his fingers. If anyone's got me figured out even a little, it's him. But I'm hoping—dear God, I'm hoping—he knows better than to say anything.

Apollo sighs. "I guess if we keep pulling her hair long enough, she might—"

"I'll send her to the Hag," I cut in. My eyes cut to Cassius. "That okay with you?"

Cassius shows me his teeth. "Pics or it didn't happen."

"Why would I be there?" I ask calmly.

"You could be, if you wanted." Reuben cuts me off. "She's a girl. Wouldn't be appropriate for you to punish her yourself."

Cassius is already nodding furiously before Reuben's done talking. "But he can watch, to make sure she receives her penance, right?"

Reuben nods.

I swallow. Hard.

This was exactly what I'd been trying to avoid.

From the first day I'd had Trinity in my class, I could tell she wasn't brittle like the countless other children who'd crossed my path the last few years.

I knew this would come to outright violence. The kind of pain and hardship people rocked in the Old Testament.

And, secretly, I'd hoped the girl would meet my expectations. Because, besides this bunch of misfits, I've never met someone I could truly regard as my equal.

She's looking to be a strong contender.

It will be a pity to break her.

"Bro, I want details," Cass says through a devilish chuckle. "I mean, blow by fucking blow." He sits forward, eyes shining. "Hear me?"

Cassius isn't a sadist.

He is, however, sitting on the fence between sociopath and psychopath.

I nod, and drop my eyes as I get to my feet. "I'll make the arrangements."

Cass lets out a laugh, clasping hands with Apollo.

Reuben watches me, silent and forever judgmental.

I guess I'm being naive thinking he doesn't have some inkling about my own dark heart. He was by my side for months before the others showed up. We're all brothers, but he's my twin. We mirror each other's darkness in different ways, but we emerged— reborn—together.

22

TRINITY

Sister Miriam leads me to the first floor of the main building. We pass several administration offices until we reach one right at the end of the hall.

There's a window. A desk. An office chair. A wooden cabinet and an old-school telephone with its receiver resting on the cradle.

It stinks of cigarettes in here, which is surprising because I didn't take Sister Miriam for a smoker. Perhaps she received a visitor that did? Was that what she was busy with while Reuben was praying for me?

She says nothing as she walks up to the wooden cabinet.

I stand in the middle of the room, not moving a hair, hoping to delay the inevitable.

As if.

She finally turns to me, a strip of leather in her hand. Broad, maybe two inches. So stiff it barely moves as she steps closer.

"Close the door."

"Sister—"

"Close the door!"

My eyes squeeze shut at her yell. I spin around and go to close the door.

When I turn, I notice a second chair. Now the cigarette smoke makes sense.

Brother Zachary Rutherford is here, smoking a cigarette. There's a low table beside him, an overflowing ashtray, and a pack of filter-less cigarettes.

He takes a drag of his cigarette, his eyes never leaving mine.

"Over here, child," Miriam calls.

"What's he doing here?"

"Making sure I do my job," she says stiffly.

From the sound of her voice, she's about to take out a week's worth of irritation on my ass.

Lashes.

In front of Zachary.

I'd beg, if I thought it would do any good. Fuck, I'd go down on my knees and pray.

I still have Reuben's rosary. Its smell has been with me all this time, but it's suddenly lost its calming effect.

"Move."

I shuffle over on wooden legs.

"Hands here," she says, using the stiff strip of leather to point to an empty space on the desk.

I press my palms to the table. I'm facing the wall, my side profile turned to Zachary.

"Feet back."

I swallow hard and scoot my feet back a few inches.

"More."

Now my ass is sticking out.

Hot, shameful tears fill my eyes. I try to blink them away, but they just end up rolling down my cheeks.

I squeeze my eyes shut when Miriam flips up my skirt. I'm

convinced she's going to tug down my underwear, but possibly to spare my modesty, she doesn't.

There's silence. Then I hear Zachary dragging on his cigarette, the dried tobacco leaves crackling faintly as they burn.

Thud.

Pain thumps into me. I gasp in surprise, vaguely proud I didn't scream.

Thud.

That wasn't so—

Thud.

I yelp in pain. Choke on a ragged sob.

Thud.

My legs go out. The pain of my knees cracking on the wooden floor is nothing compared with the dull aching throb on my ass.

This is hell.

Sister Miriam is the Devil.

She loops her arm under my waist and drags me back to my feet. "Can you stand, or does Brother Zachary need to hold you up?"

"Stop," I manage in a breathless whisper. "P-please, just stop!"

"Six more, child." There's a sudden catch in Miriam's voice. "You can do this. But you have to stand."

I manage a nod.

Thud.

I can't help it—I let out a wretched howl of pain. I'm in danger of scraping my nails off on the desk.

What could I possibly have done to deserve this?

I can end this, though, can't I?

If I tell Miriam it wasn't me.

I'll tell her to fetch Gabriel. He'll vouch. Tell him I've been set up.

Thud

Another howl, this one stronger than the last. Somehow that helps with the pain. I'm panting now; loud, ugly sounds only an animal can make. My cheeks are wet with tears. My face scrunches up as I fight the urge to collapse on the floor.

Thud

My ears start buzzing.

My legs give out.

Miriam's talking, telling me to stand.

But I can't.

I have nothing left.

An arm hoists me up. I think it's Miriam again, and that must mean she can't hit me again because—

Thud.

It's Zachary.

I can smell his slightly-sweet brand of cigarettes.

All I have to do is say his name.

Cassius.

Say it and this will stop.

She'll ask why? Why him?

I don't know.

They hate me.

Him, Apollo, Reuben.

They hate me.

But I can end this.

Nothing can be as bad as this. What will they do? More pranks? More bullying? I don't give a shit.

End this, Trinity.

Thud.

You can end this now. You just have to—

Thud.

I let out a whimpering mewl. The arm that had been

supporting me tightens. The world spins on its head, and then I'm staring up into Zachary's jade eyes.

There's something strange gleaming in them, but I don't understand it.

Thought, reasoning—not possible.

There's just pain.

It eats through me like a slow-burning fire. Like the dried tobacco in Zachary's cigarette. Ebbing and flowing but ultimately moving deeper inside me.

"Take her to her room," I hear Miriam say.

Zachary's chest rumbles against my side when he replies. "Thank you, Sister."

Miriam's voice is tight. "Make sure she puts on the salve."

That fire moves through me, consuming me. It leaves behind nothing but ash.

Zachary takes me out of the room. His chest pushes and retracts against my body. Sometimes his breath touches my face, but mostly it doesn't.

I sometimes hear voices, and sometimes just the steady thump of his feet. With every step, my body grows more and more numb.

My eyes closed moments after we left Miriam's office. I can't remember how to open them again, even when a door creaks and a strange darkness falls over me.

Zachary puts me down on something soft. On my side.

I think he lifts my skirt, but I'm not sure until something skims over my sensitive flesh. I whimper and try to move away from that touch.

"Shh," he murmurs.

The surface under me dips.

A bed.

There's the sound of a lid being opened. The strong menthol tickles my nose.

"This will hurt."

I suck in a breath as frozen fire streaks over my tender skin and I try to move away but he grabs my hip to keep me in place. Every stroke is like hot air on coals, stoking the fire buried deep within. Bringing it to the surface. I'd have started sobbing, but I'm spent.

So I lay there and somehow endure the agony.

I wish I could pray.

I wish there was someone who would listen.

I know it wouldn't change anything, but wouldn't it be nice to know you're not alone?

I'm alone.

Even here with this sadistic fuck of a man who watches while a girl is beaten black and blue and then carries her somewhere dark and secret to hurt her some more....

Even here, with him, I'm still alone.

The bed shifts.

His hand slips off the back of my neck. There's the sound of a lighter flicking. I expect cigarette smoke. But this is something else.

Pungent. Foreign.

The bed dips again.

"Open."

Something dry pokes at my lips. I part them. "Inhale."

I'm past the point of fighting this. So I do what he says and hope this is the last of it because I can't take anymore.

I'm broken and used. A grubby porcelain doll with a cracked face, left to rot in the debris of an abandoned building. Once a treasured toy, now a spider's nest.

The smoke makes me cough. But I take another drag anyway. Then again. Again. The pain is still there, but it's distant now. And fading.

No, that's me.

I'm fading.

Fingers brush my temple. A stray curl tickles the side of my ear. I let out a long breath, and my body finally relaxes.

"Who are you, Trinity Malone?"

My head thumps along with that distant pain. Something new worms its way into me. Something warm and fuzzy and…

Nice.

"No one," I murmur.

"What are you doing here?"

"Nothing."

I want to fade away completely. But he keeps asking me questions I'm compelled to answer.

"How do you know Gabriel?"

"He's my friend. My *best* friend."

There's a long pause. So long, I almost do slip away. But then those fingers come back and touch the side of my face, tracing the outline of my jaw.

"I'd really hoped that wasn't the case," Zachary says.

The bed moves as he gets up.

I'm dimly aware this might not be my room. That I'm lying on a strange bed with my underwear around my knees and the back of my skirt hitched up. My hands tremble as I reach behind me, but Zachary snatches them by the wrists before I can adjust my clothing.

"You're leaving. I'll arrange a cab for you in the morning," Zachary says. "Just give me an address."

I laugh at him. "Fuck you."

I hear the deep breath he takes, and that makes me regret what I said. But there's no address I can give him. I don't have anyone else. I don't have anywhere else.

There's a burst of dull pain as he yanks my underwear up my legs. "Sisters of Mercy it is."

Hands slide under my waist. The world spins as he scoops

me into his arms. Every thumping step he takes chafes my skin with fire.

We go down a flight of stairs, and then along a hallway. We're back on my floor, headed for room 113. He barrels through the door and drops me on the bed.

On my back.

I flip onto my side with a hiss, tears pricking at my eyelids.

"Remember, Trinity, you chose the hard way," Zachary says from the doorway. He tosses something my way, and it thumps against my tummy. Then he's gone, my bedroom door slamming shut behind him.

I fumble for the cold, hard object pressing against my stomach.

The salve.

I wrap my fingers around it and curl into a ball.

I don't cry, because there's no point. Whatever I smoked dulled the pain enough that I can probably fall asleep. But sleep doesn't come for a long time, because I keep replaying his last words to me.

You chose the hard way.

Just remember, Trinity.

You chose the hard way.

23

ZAC

"Morning, Boss."

I look up and frown at Cassius. It takes me a few seconds to move after the shock of seeing him at my door so early in the morning. "The fuck you doing?" I hiss, lurching across the room, hauling him inside, and shutting the door quietly behind him.

First Reuben, now this? You'd swear everyone had a fucking brain aneurysm this week with how they've been acting.

"How'd it go?"

"You couldn't wait?" I swipe a hand through my hair. "This is far from fucking circumspect."

"Circumspect," Cassius repeats under his breath, his eyes moving away from mine. "Smells dank in here. You still got that fatty around?"

"Cassius, you have to leave!" I hurriedly lower my voice. "No one can see you in my room."

"Why?" He drags a finger over my desk as if inspecting it for dust. "They'd just think we were fucking."

He's immaculately dressed this morning. Could be the cooler

weather—those same clouds that keep threatening are gathering force—that made him put on his blazer, but there's no possible explanation for his perfect tie.

I grab the sleeve of his jacket and twist the fabric, using that grip to turn him around. "Look at me," I snap when his eyes slide away from mine.

"Relax, Boss." He drawls.

I hurriedly release him and step back. "How are you feeling, Cass?" I ask warily.

We start a dance, him and I. He moves to the left, I slide to the right. Round and round we go, where we'll stop, nobody knows.

"Honestly? A little left out." He sends a sparkling smile my way. "See, the last time we spoke, you laid out this brilliant fucking plan—" he waves a hand "—like you always do, and I was legit salivating to hear how it all played out."

He stops and pulls open the top drawer of my desk. I let him —I have nothing to hide from my brothers. If we still felt the need to keep secrets after the shit we went through then we'd be more fucked in the head than any psychology handbook could explain.

"You didn't call. You said you'd call." Cass looks up and lifts out the half-finished blunt I'd stowed away last night. "Feels like I got stood up."

"She got her lashes. I gave her a way out, she didn't take it. What more do you want to know?"

Cassius sinks down on my bed and lights the joint.

Gritting my teeth, I lurch forward and snatch it from his lips before the flame can touch the paper. "This hall gets foot traffic in an hour. The smell won't be gone by then."

"You know what doesn't get traffic?" Cassius leans back on my bed, propping himself up on his elbows. "My fucking dick.

Not once since we've been here. I have needs, Boss. There's only so much wanking one dick can—"

He cuts off when I slam my drawer shut, the joint tossed back inside. "Stop acting like a fucking kid," I snap.

"Yeah?" He sits forward in a rush. "You know I don't have this mental fucking switch I can just turn off like you fuckers." He rests back on his elbows again. "You *know* that."

I study him for a second, and then lean to the side to turn the digital alarm clock to face me. "Fine," I say through a sigh. "Move over."

I hesitate, and then check the clock again. Then I lean over and snag the joint from my drawer, lighting it in one go. If I keep my door closed a little longer and open the window, most of the smell should have dissipated before the staff start moving around.

"So she walks into Miriam's office—"

"**W**ill you tell that bedtime story to me every night?" Cass says, beaming up at me with a goofy grin. About halfway through the retelling he settled down onto my bed, head resting on his hands.

"Sure," I say through a chuckle. "But now you have to get out of here." My eyes move to the digital alarm clock. "Because this really is the worst time for us to have to try and explain shit."

"Yeah, yeah." He pushes up onto his elbows, but then he pauses. "Hey, Zac?"

I pause, rendered frozen by the hesitation in his voice. "What?"

"If you were fucked in the head, do you think you'd know it right away?"

My hackles rise, but I do my best to keep my expression disinterested. "Like, if you went insane?"

"Yeah, sure. Like that. Do you think you'd know?"

I bring up my leg, but I put it down when I realize I was going to start rubbing my ankle. "It depends. If you're schizo, then probably not. Because it's so real to you, and you'd commonly start to disassociate."

"So your friends wouldn't pick up on it either?" he adds.

We've all learned a few things about the human mind. While I find it fascinating enough to possibly get my Masters in it one day, the Brotherhood approach it like other guys might football. Something we're all familiar with, and it passes the time.

"Depends on the level of the delusions you suffer. Bipolar, that's a different story. Relationships are the first to suffer, because you're not exactly antisocial. Borderline—"

"I almost fucked her."

My head dips forward before I can straighten my neck. "Her...Trinity?" My eyebrows shoot up to my fucking hairline.

After I *specifically* fucking forbade him from—

"It was before you said anything. She just got here." Cassius scrapes his nails over his buzz cut. "Before we knew she was...important."

I force myself to take a deep breath. "But you didn't, right?"

He stays quiet.

"*Right?*"

"I almost did."

"But you didn't."

"No."

"Then we're fine."

I didn't say he was fine. He wasn't.

None of us were.

"I'm sorry."

"You didn't know."

"Yeah, but, fuuuck. I *almost*…"

My skin goes numb. I wasn't listening right. I thought he was feeling guilty about my command not to try and sleep with Trinity before we'd figured out if she were a threat or not…but that wasn't it, was it?

"Cass."

"Yeah, I fucking know." He sits up in a rush. "Jesus." He scratches at his scalp with his nails.

I put a hand on his knee. "That doesn't mean you're…"

What the fuck am I supposed to say? He almost raped her, and I'm supposed to tell him everything's okay? I might sound like I know shit, but I don't have a fucking clue if this means he's a cunt hair away from becoming a serial rapist or if he's as frustrated as the rest of us.

Would anyone know?

Is the brain truly that predictable?

Now that we have the vague approximations of blueprints from deviants like Gacy and Bundy, can human nature honestly be read like a fucking deck of cards?

"Let's…we're just taking this one step at a time, all right?"

That was our motto back then when we were holed up in that cold, rat-infested basement.

One day at a time.

Dawn was our alarm clock. The Universe's equivalent of a reset button. When dawn crept in through those gap-toothed boards and ran a slow scan down the dusty floor where they kept us…it was a new day.

A day filled with possibilities.

And always, a day filled with horror.

A bell sounds. I peel open my eyes with difficulty as I shift a body weighing ten tons.

What time is it?

What *day* is it?

I'm dimly aware a lot of time has passed since Zachary laid me on my bed. The pain woke me up a few times since then, but I only stayed awake long enough to nurse my bruises with ointment. Surprisingly, no one's bothered me. I guess Miriam had no choice but to give me a sick day.

I lie here in the dark, wincing as I fumble for the jar. I screw open the lid and scoop out some salve.

It stings going on but not nearly as much as yesterday. My bruises are healing but my pride is still battered and blue.

It seems so stupid not telling them about Cassius's drawing. I can't fight against the certainty he'll do something even worse if I rat him out. After all, what's stopping him from sneaking into my room and finishing what he started?

I'd love to know what I did to earn this. I mean, I've heard of hazing but does everyone really go through this when they arrive here?

I've heard of bullying too, but nothing like this.

I set down the jar on my side of the desk. There's barely enough moonlight coming in through the window to make out Jasper's body humping up the blankets on his bed.

I really, *really* need to pee.

I don't even bother sitting on the edge of the bed. I go straight to my feet, grimacing when my skirt brushes over my underwear.

Lord, this hurts. The worst I've ever gotten from Mom was a slap on my rump with her bare hand when I threw a tantrum. I think I was like ten or something.

Dad never laid a hand on me. He'd wanted to once, but my mother had stopped him. I can't even remember what I'd done wrong.

It's pretty late though, right? If Jasper's here and asleep, then it has to be sometime after ten.

Pretty sure I'm the only one awake on this floor. Which means I'd have the bathroom all to myself.

It's gonna hurt to go shower. But at least I'll be sure no one's going to walk in on me. And maybe the hot water will soothe out the pain.

I take out some pajamas, clean underwear, socks. I ease open the door and check the hallway before stepping outside.

Then I hesitate.

I thought Father Gabriel would come see me yesterday, but the only person I saw was Jasper. I could go there now. To Father Gabriel's room. I could tell him what happened.

Everything.

He said I'm safe here, and look what's happened? I've been bullied and falsely accused without a say in the matter.

Would he honestly let that happen?

A few minutes later, I'm standing in front of Father Gabriel's door. It takes every ounce of courage I have to knock. I'm still not convinced I can tell him everything, but I'm craving his comfort. I need someone to hold me and tell me everything's going to be okay.

Like a toddler with a boo-boo. Real mature, Trinity.

My knock sounds too loud in this broad, empty hallway.

But obviously, it isn't loud enough because there's no response.

I try again.

My hand goes over the doorknob. Locked.

Ha. So much for him trusting his things are safe. I guess that only applies to orphans like me who don't have anything valuable to steal.

I step back, bristling with a sudden anger.

I'm about to give the door the finger when movement catches my eye.

Reuben walks down the hallway. I stiffen, and like the idiot I am, I don't even think of fleeing.

"He's not here," Reuben says.

"Yeah, I figured."

"He'll be back tomorrow."

"You his PA or something?"

There's not a hint of what he might be thinking in those black eyes. "Or something," he says. "You should be in your room." His eyes dart down to the clothes bundled up in my arm. "What are you doing up here?"

I'm not big on lies. My mother had a good nose for them, and she'd catch me out every time. It was easier to tell her the truth. But lies come easier when you're dealing with strangers. The past few weeks have been a learning curve for me.

I'm fine.

No, I don't need to speak to a counselor.

Yes, I've said my prayers.

I'm still the furthest thing from a conman, but I'm pretty sure I sound convincing when I say, "Father Gabriel said I could use his bathroom so I don't have to share with the boys." I cross my arms, lifting my chin as I mentally dare Reuben to see through my lie. "But he forgot to leave me his key. Do you have one?"

The faintest smile touches Reuben's generous mouth. "I wish I did."

"Well, then, it's pointless us standing here, isn't it?" I put on my iciest expression and swing around to leave.

A hand closes around my shoulder and turns me back. I wince as my skirt shifts against my sensitive backside. But I smooth away the pained look before Reuben can notice.

"You should be careful around him," Reuben says.

"Father Gabriel?" I laugh. "You know he's a bishop, right?"

"Not anymore." Reuben dips his head, and the dim lighting in the hallway casts pools of shadows in his eye sockets. "And even if he still was, titles don't mean anything around here."

"I'm sure the *provost* thinks different." I snatch my shoulder away from his fingers and take a quick step back.

He doesn't try and touch me again, but his eyes fall to my chest instead.

Ugh. Why are men so disgusting? They see anything with boobs, and they can't seem to think straight.

I whirl around and hurry down the hall as fast as my sore ass allows. Just before I take the stairs, I glance back over my shoulder.

The hallway is empty.

Reuben is gone.

TRINITY

My footsteps echo hollowly as I head for the closest shower stall. I stopped to use the restroom on the way here, and everywhere I went it was like walking through a frozen world.

There's a strange hush in Saint Amos this late at night. As if the building itself is sleeping too.

Or waiting.

There's a chance Reuben might still be stalking the halls. Heaven knows what he was doing on Father Gabriel's floor to begin with. Maybe him and Cassius work in shifts. But I'm pretty sure he has better things to do than stalk me.

I force a smile.

It doesn't help.

I shiver, and look over my shoulder.

A quick shower, and then back in bed. There's no way Sister Miriam will let me take another day off—I'm going to need all the restorative sleep I can get. I wish I had more of whatever it was Zachary gave me to smoke. It worked tons better than the salve.

It was weed, wasn't it? Because I'm pretty sure you smoke crack through a glass pipe or something.

I turn on the shower.

Icy water splashes down, making me squeal in surprise and snatch away my hand.

The water becomes lukewarm, then hot.

Yes!

I pull my dress over my head with a wince, and toss it on the floor. My dry clothes are stacked on the far side of the cubicle wall. Close enough that I don't have to walk naked across the whole room to dress, but far enough so they don't get wet.

The shift is next. I step out of my undies and give them a quick inspection. No blood on the back—guess I'm just bruised after all. I wish there were a mirror in this place, but they're as sparse as they were back at my house.

With a hard swallow, I try and prepare myself for the coming pain.

There's a noise behind me.

I whirl around, covering my breasts as I scan the empty room. I should hurry, unless I want some random boy walking in on me.

The right side door swings open causing my breath to catch in my throat.

No.

Reuben enters the bathroom.

No!

I snatch up my clothes and hurriedly slip into my underwear as I yell, "Hey! Get out!"

He doesn't even slow down.

"I swear, I'll scream!"

The door opens again. My eyes flit over to it as I grab my top and tug it over my head.

Cassius swaggers into the room, his eyes already on me.

Where Reuben is staring at me like an obstacle he plans walking straight through, Cassius is mentally peeling back the clothes I'm throwing on with trembling hands.

Reuben stops a foot away from where the tiles begin. Just standing there, staring at me. *Through* me. Cassius joins him. "You're right, Rube. She's definitely not supposed to be here."

What the hell is going on?

Cassius steps closer. "You could get in all sorts of trouble being outside your room this late at night." He yanks away my sweatpants before I can tug them up my legs.

Right, because he's the fucking *hallway monitor.*

Oh my God. What's wrong with these people?

"Now what are we going to do about this transgression?" He takes another step, and I throw my hands up.

"Touch me and I'll scream."

"Do it," Cassius says. "No one can hear you. Not down here."

I back up, flinching when my back touches the wall. It's way too cold through the thin fabric of my vest "I'll tell Father Gabriel about this. And about the drawing." My eyes flicker to Reuben, but he could have been watching clouds moving across the sky for all the emotion on his face. "And I'll tell him about what you did on Monday."

Cassius cocks his head. "Compulsive liar much?" He leans to the side, grabbing hold of the edge of the tiled cubicle wall. Then he slowly starts unlacing his shoe.

I bare my teeth at him, inching to the side. If he moves closer and Reuben stays where he is, then I could squeeze past them. I'm not an athlete, but I'm sure I'm faster than them.

Would have been splendid if you'd been all soaped up and naked, don't you think? Like trying to catch a greased pig. Except you've got clothes on, Genius.

Cassius straightens and toes off his shoes. Then he pulls his shirt over his head.

Even in my panicked state, I can't help but notice his slim, perfectly proportioned body. Porcelain skin—not even a freckle to mar it. A dusting of hair trails from his chest down a flat, hard stomach and disappears behind his trunks.

"Reuben, can you move?" a voice calls out. "You're blocking my shot."

Reuben twists around, revealing Apollo. He's standing by the bench, his video camera trained on me.

My eyes want to pop out of their sockets.

"What the hell?" I breathe.

Cassius unbuttons his slacks, the rasp of the zipper drawing my eyes back to him. "Since you can't seem to take a hint, you little hussy, we've decided to stop being so fucking subtle."

"You're not supposed to touch her," Reuben says, turning disapproving eyes on Cassius.

Cassius throws him an irritated look which melts away as soon as he focuses on me again. I'm crowded into the corner now, a steaming waterfall between us.

"Please," I say, lifting my hands again. "Just let me go."

"Oh, we *want* you to go." Cassius shows me his teeth, but he's not smiling. "That's the fucking point. But you seem incapable of putting two and two together."

He steps out of his pants.

His black form-fitting trunks leave nothing to the imagination. I've never seen one before, but I'm pretty sure he has an erection. To my virgin eyes, it looks abnormally long and thick.

Panic transforms into anger.

How dare they? How fucking *dare* they? Honest to God, do they really think they'll get away with this? That I won't say something?

Without thinking, I scramble up the low wall. The adrenaline pumping through me puts wings on my feet, because I didn't even know if I could get over—and then I'm landing on the other side with a slap of bare feet.

I race for the door.

Apollo drops his video camera and chases after me.

Blood sings in my ears as I grab the door handle and wrench it open.

But there's someone blocking my way.

I bounce off Zachary's chest and land with a pained yelp on the floor. I'm up a second later, turning around and stabbing a finger toward Cassius.

"He...he was going to—to—"

Apollo skids to a halt, raising his hands like I'm pointing a gun.

Cassius turns to face the door, props his elbow on the cubicle wall, and rests his chin on his palm. "Christ, Zac, what took you so fucking long?"

None of the guys look like they've been caught assaulting a female student.

None of them even look remotely guilty.

Which means...

I turn, my eyes going wide. My heart's about to explode in my chest.

Zachary steps into the bathroom and closes the door behind him.

Then he locks it.

2 6

ZAC

What *took* me so long? I came as soon as I got his fucking message. I scan the room, taking a snapshot of the situation. Trinity tries to dart past me, but I catch the back of her vest and haul her back.

That vest and a pair of white panties is all she's wearing.

I sling an arm around her throat and put her in a lock. Not enough to choke her. Not even enough to cut off oxygen to her brain. Though I should have if I'd known how much trouble she'd be.

"This wasn't what we agreed," I drag Trinity forward with me despite her struggles. She sinks her nails into my arm, but even when she draws blood I barely feel it.

The ache in my wrists and ankles though? That's another story. That shit's been keeping me up at night. Getting high is the only thing that keeps it at bay lately.

When she starts gasping and gagging like I'm actually strangling her, I slap her ass. She yelps, whimpers, and goes still. I expect her to start bawling like a little girl, but her only response is a hitched breath.

"I told you to keep her contained until I arrived."

Cassius waves a hand at the shower cubicle. "Container." Then, he leans over and turns off the water. "In which she was contained up until a second ago."

I shake my head through a long-suffering stare. "Where are the ropes and—?"

At this, the girl lets out an indignant gasp and starts struggling again. Another smack on her ass shuts her up as abruptly as the first time. Her knees give out, but I just drag her up again.

"And the gag?"

She screams.

I haul her up against my chest and clap a hand over her mouth. No one lives on this level and the walls are thick, but we can't risk someone hearing the commotion.

How could we possibly explain away any of this?

Apollo moves closer. He holds out some cable ties constructed into a set of handcuffs. "No one uses ropes anymore, Zac," he says, rolling his eyes as he cuffs Trinity's wrists in front of her while I keep her mouth shut with my hand.

My ankles and wrists ache in protest at that comment, but I don't challenge him. "And the gag?"

Apollo shrugs.

"Here," Cassius says, jogging up to us. What the hell happened to his clothes? "Nothing like some used panties to shut a girl up."

Trinity struggles in my arms, whimpering against my hand.

Not exactly hygienic, but there are worse things in life.

Much, *much* worse.

I ball up her stale panties and shove them into her mouth.

She spits them out.

I give Cassius a deadpan stare. He rolls his eyes at me and

steps toward Reuben, gesturing at his crotch. Reuben lifts his arms like he's being frisked while Cassius yanks off his belt.

He takes Rube's belt, plucks Trinity's panties from the floor, balls them up, and shoves them back into her mouth.

Then he uses the belt to keep them in place, tightening the buckle at the back of her neck.

Apollo comes back to the group, face forlorn. "I broke my camera," he whines.

"I'll buy you a new one," I say, without looking away from Trinity.

"Hmm," Cassius murmurs as he presses himself against Trinity. "Do we have to leave right now, Boss? Couldn't we have a little fun with her first?"

"Cut it out," I snap.

Astronauts can see his hard-on from the fucking moon. I cock my head toward him, making eye contact with Reuben. "Thought I told you to keep an eye on him?"

For once, Reuben doesn't stay quiet. He shrugs. "We were waiting for you."

The *fuck*?

The last thing I need is Reuben crushing on this chick. She's already done possibly irreparable damage to our brotherhood—which I'll make her pay dearly for—but this is a knock we don't need.

Apollo comes closer, his broken camera dangling from his hand. He starts studying Trinity like he's never seen a girl before and then steps back with a grimace. "Can we at least clean her up before we go? She really needs a shower."

Trinity widens her eyes at him.

Was that what I was smelling? My nose wrinkles before I can stop myself.

"Yeah. Just a quick wash," Cass murmurs close to my ear.

When did he come up behind me? He's got cat's feet sometimes, the evil shit.

Trinity shrieks behind the gag and yanks herself free. I wasn't holding onto her all that tight—where the fuck would she go, anyway? The door's locked.

She stumbles, probably not expecting to get free so easily, and goes to her knees with a muffled yelp.

"Don't you wanna see what's under there?" Cass is right against me now, whispering into my ear like the fucking devil himself. Another inch, and his dick will be poking my leg.

I shove my shoulder back, pushing him away. "That's not why we're here."

Trinity scrambles up, spinning around to glare at Cass and me. She frowns furiously at us as she works to loosen the belt with her bound hands.

I'd caught a glimpse of her ass when Miriam was giving her those lashes yesterday afternoon. It took every ounce of self-control I could muster not to get more than a semi. Especially when her sweet howls of pain echoed around me. When I'd taken her to my room after I'd specifically not lit a candle. But it hadn't been fully dark yet so I'd still gotten a fantastic view of her bruised ass when I'd put on the lotion.

I'd had just as much difficulty stopping myself from squeezing that ass. From slipping off my clothes and having her bare skin flush with mine.

"It's two in the fucking morning," Cass says. He's moved closer again. "No one's gonna come."

Before Trinity can loosen the belt, Reuben steps up behind her. He slides an arm around her waist and snags the cuffs, pulling her hands away. She freezes, eyes wide and sparkling with fear. He hooks a finger into the cable ties and shifts his grip so he's keeping her close with the same arm.

"We can't, Cass," I say in a low voice. "It's…"

Wrong.

Stupid.

Juvenile.

Reuben strokes her neck. At least, that's what I think he's doing. I lean back a little.

What the fuck?

He tugs, and a red rosary slips out from behind Trinity's vest. He nestles it carefully between her breasts.

Fuck, that's his rosary, isn't it? He *does* like her.

This is the last thing we need.

But who the fuck am I to deny us the things we so desperately need?

"You have five minutes."

Cassius darts past me, slapping Apollo's shoulder as he passes. "Rube, bring her!"

Trinity's eyes are bugging out of her head. She'd been keeping perfectly still while Reuben rearranged her jewelry, like a small fluffy animal trying to camouflage itself from a predator.

Only one problem.

There are four of us, and only one of her.

She can't hide. She can't even run.

She'll have to endure it. Which could prove to be a dear lesson for her.

We've had many such lessons and they've only made us stronger.

We'd be making her stronger too.

She catches my eye, and her skin pales.

Why?

I guess it's my smile.

27

TRINITY

T his can't be happening.

It's not real.

This is all just another prank. They're going to shove me under the showerhead, maybe wet my hair. A little roughhousing. That's it.

They wouldn't *dare*.

Would they?

A shiver chases through me, spilling goosebumps over my skin and hardening my nipples under my thin vest. Reuben tosses me over his shoulder like a sack of potatoes, knocking the air from my lungs and leaving me momentarily stunned.

By the time I recover, I'm already in the shower cubicle. The shower's already on, steam churning into the air.

Too hot. It's too fucking hot!

Someone's chuckling under their breath. It's fucking terrifying.

I wriggle and scream into my gag as loud as I can when Reuben grabs my hips and sets me back on my feet. When I try to run, Zachary catches me with an arm and shoves me back. Cass grabs my cuffs and reels me in like a fish.

Water hits my hands, then my arms. It's not as hot as I'd thought, but it's warmer than I like. I struggle furiously, but that makes the plastic ties cut into my wrists.

That shit hurts, so I stop.

I could vault the wall again, but what would that help? I saw Zachary lock the door. The key is in the pocket of his slacks and—

I peek around at the sound of a belt buckle. Zachary unhooks his belt. His penetrating green eyes catching mine when he looks up.

This *is* real. This *is* happening. They don't give a fuck about the consequences.

My knees sag.

I'd have landed on my ass if Cassius hadn't caught my elbow and steadied me. "Aw...You done fighting?" he asks. "I was enjoying that."

"She knows it will be over sooner if she doesn't resist," Zachary says as he steps out of his shoes. He slips his shirt over the top of his head without bothering to undo the buttons.

There's a tattoo on his chest.

A coiling serpent. Fangs bared, ready to strike.

Oh my fucking God.

He steps out of his pants, baring white cotton boxers as plain as my own underwear.

Reuben steps away, turns his back, and slips off his own shirt.

This isn't happening.

I shriek into my gag and try to jerk free from Cassius. Pain slices through my wrists, and a tiny rivulet of blood races down my arm. Water hits it, turning it pink and then invisible in a flash.

Apollo hangs back. He's still chuckling, but he seems content to stand back while they...

Wash me?

Shame bursts through me. My chest tightens painfully.

"You're hurting her," Reuben says.

My eyes fly back to him. I'd been watching Apollo, trying to plead with him. He doesn't seem willing to participate, so it's worth a shot, right?

But staring at him means I can't keep an eye on the other three.

An arm slips around my chest. Cassius drags me against him and a hard length presses into the small of my back.

I don't want to look, but I have to. Else how will I spot my chance at escape?

Zachary's still smiling. I think it's the first time I've ever seen him look anything other than dead serious. "Take off the gag. We don't want to waterboard her."

Expert fingers manipulate the buckle at the back of my neck. The belt slips loose before he plucks it away. I spit out my underwear and haul in a sweet breath.

Relief only lasts a second.

Cassius pushes me forward. Water cascades over my head.

Blinded by the water, with Cassius's arm still securely around my waist, I don't stand a chance.

I can dimly make out Zachary with his dark smudge of a tattoo. He grabs a bar of soap and lathers it in his hands as he moves closer.

Cassius shoves me forward. My bound hands stick out on instinct, slamming into Zachary's chest. I puncture him with my nails, but he doesn't even flinch.

While I'm still spitting water out of my mouth, he shoves his hands under my vest and starts washing me.

I gasp, twisting to try and get away from his hands. But

they're everywhere—my stomach, my breasts, my armpits, my back.

That's when Reuben steps up to us. He's easily an inch taller than Zachary, but he doesn't push him aside. Instead, he grabs the back of my neck and my arm, holding me still for Zachary.

"Please," I whisper, forcing myself to look at Zachary.

When we lock eyes, an electrical current surges through me. There's no sympathy in his eyes. Not even a trace of pity. He's enjoying this.

Is it my fear or my humiliation that gets him hard?

"You had your chance," he says. "You could have been out of here this morning already."

I open my mouth to tell him I'll leave, but then Cassius turns off the shower. There's a moment's crystallized silence, broken only by the *plink* of a water drop hitting the wet tiles.

Zachary tilts his head a little, daring me to speak. When I say nothing, he slides a hand over my breast and squeezes.

Hard.

I suppress a gasp, and will my eyes to stay on his.

Begging did nothing. Neither did threatening to rat on them. But maybe showing them I still have a backbone will make them think twice about taking this too far.

Zachary's eyes narrow.

He doesn't like that I'm defying him.

Another hand grazes up the back of my vest, tracing my spine. I break out in goosebumps, my nipples going hard again.

Terror dulls into something else.

He was right—the less I struggle, the faster this will go.

My breath hitches when the hand sliding down my back slips behind my underwear. Soaked from the shower, everything clings to me. I grimace when Cassius tugs down my wet underwear to my knees.

Hot breath tickles my ear. "Who'd have thought you'd be

such a dirty girl?" Cassius asks. "You should be thanking us, you know? Working so hard to get you clean."

Reuben releases me. Maybe it's because I'm standing still now. Maybe it's because he knows—like I do—that there's no chance of me escaping again. "We can protect you," he says, making absolutely zero fucking sense.

"Shut the fuck up," Cassius snaps. He moves back a little, and his voice changes direction. "Why don't you go stand there by Apollo?"

I shiver at the sudden loss of heat. Without the shower on, the air is cooling rapidly. Reuben steps back, but he doesn't leave.

Zachary starts washing me again. The sensation of his soapy hands gliding over my skin makes my insides squirm.

It should be in fear, in revulsion, in anger.

But something else is blooming inside me. Something hot and tingly. It builds deep between my legs like a well that's slowly filling up with rainwater.

Zachary must sense something, because his smile fades. "She's clean enough." His eyes flicker away from mine. "Let's rinse her."

Cassius does as Zachary commands.

I flinch when hot water hits my back and then gasp when Cassius's hand slides down my tender ass and slips between my legs.

I lift onto my toes.

Now the only sound is the thumping water.

He cups my pussy.

Like an animal catching scent of its prey, Zachary's nostrils flare. His gaze skims down my body, settling on the hand between my legs.

His voice is low and so, so deep. "Cass...don't."

Cassius turns off the water, but he keeps his hand where it is. "I want to know if you're wet for us," he murmurs into my ear.

My eyes flutter as I try to stand even taller. My legs start shaking. I worm my fingers up Zachary's chest. Grabbing onto his shoulder, I tighten my grip until he looks at me.

I blink furiously, lick my lips, and mouth, "Please," at him.

That was the wrong thing to say.

"Well?" he murmurs, his breath stirring against my wet skin. His voracious eyes flicker up to Cassius. "Is she?"

Cassius groans like he's in pain. There's the unmistakable sound of wet fabric sliding against skin. His warm, hard cock presses against my thigh.

I whimper and dig my nails into Zachary's shoulder muscles. "Don't." The word comes out like a bullet. "Don't do this."

The hand between my leg clenches. I gasp and stagger forward until I'm flush with Zachary's hot, dry skin. The move should have dislodged Cassius's hand, but he moves with me.

Now I'm sandwiched between him and Zachary.

I've been appealing to the wrong person. He's obviously in charge, but it's as if he's been derailed.

Or maybe he's okay with this.

The thought makes me sick to my stomach.

So why are there electric tingles skating over my skin?

Is it because I've never had a hard body pressed against mine, never mind two? Because I've never looked up into eyes as intensely hungry as Zachary's? Or had a man touch me the way Cassius is touching me now?

In a normal situation, I'd have dated any of these guys in a heartbeat.

But normal isn't what got me to Saint Amos.

In this room, normal isn't a part of anyone's vocabulary.

We're all fucked in the head. I should be repelled by these men, but their presence is like a magnet to my leaden heart.

The wickedness of this sick, twisted moment feels so fucking right.

My eyelids grow heavy. I lean in, fully expecting Zachary to close the distance and kiss me.

A hand slithers over my ass and wedges between Cassius and me.

And then squeezes.

I yelp with pain. My eyes fly open.

Grim desire gleams in Zachary's eyes, now so dark green they could be black. His lips part as if he wants to say something.

Someone rattles the bathroom door.

I jump. Everyone spins to face the door.

Another rattle, this one harder than the last.

Then quiet.

Behind me, another drop of water plinks onto the tiles.

"Time to go," Zachary says.

"Yeah, no shit." Cassius withdraws, leaving me stranded on the tiles.

I start shivering. Reuben happens to glance at me as he slips his shirt over his head. He moves up beside me and drapes the towel I brought with me over my shoulders.

"How we gonna leave without someone seeing?" Apollo asks, hugging himself as he looks from me to Zachary.

"One at a time." Zachary looks back at me, and then his eyes move to Reuben.

"Bring her."

28

ZAC

My mind's reeling. I don't know who rattled the door, but thank fuck they did. Shit was about to get out of hand, and in a big way.

I was so close to losing control, I can still taste mint in my mouth. That would always happen back then when I lost myself in the moment.

We all found ways to deal with the shit we went through. I absorbed everything like a sponge. But there was no one to squeeze me out. That shit stayed inside me and festered into something dark and perverse.

I thought I had a handle on it.

Fuck, I think we all thought that until this girl arrived, all pure and innocent and shit.

Like dropping a mouse into a pit of hungry vipers.

"What are you waiting for?" I click my fingers. "Bring her."

Reuben blinks like he's coming out of a trance. Then he scoops up Trinity and throws her over his shoulder.

I take my keys out of my pocket and toss them to Apollo. "Make sure the coast is clear."

He nods and hustles outside with his broken camera under his arm, leaving the door to swing closed behind him. I happen to look at Cass, and we lock eyes for a moment. I don't expect guilt or remorse. Most of us aren't capable of expressing those emotions anymore. What I don't expect is the brief flash of uncertainty.

I give Apollo a few seconds to check the hallway, and then beckon the guys after me as I make for the door.

We don't encounter anyone else on our way to the exit. Whoever had tried to enter the bathroom had disappeared. Maybe one of the younger guys had wet their bed or something. That kind of shit happens a lot around here.

Apollo's waiting for us at the door leading to the northern grounds. Soon as I give him a nod, he runs to the crypt.

I wait a few seconds, and then slap Reuben on the shoulder not currently occupied by the bound and gagged girl we'd almost fucked in the showers.

Trinity lifts her head anyway and glares amber daggers at me.

Fuck, but she's beautiful, even with Reuben's belt between her teeth. Probably *especially* because she's fucking gagged.

In class she'd been meek and submissive—the perfect prey. But she showed me her teeth tonight, if only for a moment. It had roused the animal in all of us. Self-control, morals, revenge —for a few minutes nothing existed except our new toy.

Will I ever get to play with her again?

I grab her chin and brush her skin with my thumb.

Not a chance. It's too easy to lose control around her. Too easy to make a mistake. We haven't gotten this far for someone like her to fuck this all up.

Reuben breaks that brief contact as he steps forward and breaks into a trot. Cass and I stay behind, waiting for him to get clear.

"Ever wonder what'll happen when Rube gets mad?" Cassius

murmurs as he squeezes into the doorway beside me. "I mean like really, really mad?"

"Like when he comes face to face with his Ghost?"

Of course I've wondered. That imaginary scene of chaotic violence has been the focus of some of my best jerk-off sessions.

"Yeah. Like that," Cassius says before jogging across the grounds.

I follow after a beat.

Reuben is only a few yards from the crypt entrance when we arrive. When he throws open the door, there's nothing but pitch black beyond. Apollo hurries forward and holds open the door for me, giving me a mock salute when I step through.

He doesn't follow us inside.

His job is to make sure we aren't disturbed.

Reuben's already halfway down the library's easternmost aisle when I reach the basement level of the crypt. Cassius trails him, toying with Trinity's hair as they walk. People come down here so rarely there's a layer of dust over everything. That's why we make sure to tread where we least suspect someone will notice our footprints.

Over the months and years we've been enrolled at Saint Amos—and especially after I got my first set of keys as a teacher — we've managed to carve out a space of our own. Back here, far out of sight, we've arranged a few of the bookshelves so it looks as if the library ends a few yards short.

The ground floor of the crypt is for short meetings. This place, on the other hand…it's our nest. A sacred space no one knows exists. The only way in is through a gap hidden by a drape.

Reuben stands there now, holding Trinity's upper arm.

Now that she's back on her feet, Trinity seems to be a touch calmer than before. Or it could be the books. They have a calming effect on us too. The same hush seems to fill every library in the world fills this one too.

"Go ahead," I tell Reuben as I grasp Trinity's other arm. "We're right behind you."

He shrugs his shoulders, pushes aside the thick drape, and miraculously makes himself disappear into that dark sliver.

Cassius follows, and then sticks out a hand for Trinity. She resists a little at first, and then throws me a furious look when I make the kind of soothing sounds you use to calm a skittish horse. With a chuckle, I feed her through the gap, Cassius pulling her from the other side.

Unlike us, she goes through easily.

Too easily.

If we don't pay attention, she could escape.

Good thing Apollo's keeping watch upstairs then.

Reuben turns on the lamp as I slide through the gap. Warm orange light suffuses the nest. From Trinity's wide eyes and stiff form, I'm guessing she didn't expect anything like this.

The space is as large as the library is wide, which is about ten yards, give or take. We've split our nest into two areas—a pseudo living area with sofas, chairs, and tables, and a makeshift bedroom.

Thankfully, since we all have private rooms in the dormitory, no one notices if we don't sleep in that wretched building, especially if we make sure we're back inside before first light.

The bedroom area is separated by another stolen drape. At

the moment, it's tucked off to one side, baring the layers of mattresses and blankets and pillows that make up that side of the room.

A true nest.

And I guess Trinity's mind comes to the worst possible conclusion when she sees it.

She shrieks through her gag and races straight for the gap in the bookshelves. I catch the first thing I can, and yank her back by a handful of wet curls.

Reuben takes off his shirt, staring at the damp spot she made with no expression. He grabs a fresh shirt from the pile neatly stacked on one of the numerous bookshelves we used to create this space.

We moved out most of the books from this side of the wall and replaced them with bottles of sacramental wine and hard booze, cartons of cigarettes, porn magazines, and whatever else we felt we couldn't keep in the dorm.

I haven't been down here in close to a week. I'm not sure when last one of my brothers was either. We've been avoiding this space, and each other, so we wouldn't risk exposing ourselves.

We were so close, too.

I tighten the fist in Trinity's hair.

So fucking close.

I turn her to face me, and then wrench open the belt keeping her gag in place. For once, she doesn't spit out her panties immediately. Instead, she watches me with wide, bright eyes as her lips tremble an inch apart.

"The next time you run, I'm taking you over my knee. Do you understand?"

She hesitates, and then nods.

Cassius is close—I can feel his body heat. From the sounds of things, Reuben is pouring us shots.

I could use one.

I could use a blunt even more, but that's Cass's department. "Roll us one," I tell him. He moves away, taking his warmth with him.

I stick a finger in Trinity's mouth, hook her underwear and yank it out. She licks her lips and grimaces, but then smooths her face.

"You're hurting me," she says.

"What's your point?"

Something flickers in her eyes. Fear? Panic? It's gone too fast for me to make out.

I can't imagine what she's thinking. Luckily for her, she's not going to be wondering about anything for much longer.

29

TRINITY

This place looks like a psycho's version of a man cave with all the dirty magazines and alcohol lying around. The sofas have seen better years—most have been duct-taped to stop the stuffing from coming out.

Then again, it is clean, if untidy. No rat droppings or cockroaches anywhere.

And not a single mote of dust.

A stark contrast with the library I walked through to get here. I can't believe this place was here the whole time I'd been teaching Jasper. I didn't have a clue. Which I suppose is exactly what they made sure of.

Zachary still has a hand in my hair. His tight grip stings, but the ties around my wrists hurt more.

There's no way in hell I'm giving up on running out of here because he threatened to smack my bottom. Draw me over his knee? He'll have to fucking catch me first, won't he? Do they honestly think I didn't notice how difficult it was for them to get inside this place?

Especially Reuben.

I'll be out the door before they make it to the stairs.

Except for Apollo, who's obviously guarding the door upstairs.

But everyone's on edge right now. It shows in their eyes. I need them to let down their guard. I do my best not to let Zachary in on the fact I'm watching Reuben pouring alcohol into some mismatched tumblers and glasses.

Let them drink and be fucking merry.

Soon as they're not paying attention, I'm out of here.

Zachary inhales a huge breath. His eyes haven't left me once since I tried to run out. And that was my first mistake. I should have waited for the right time. But I'd seen this place, and I'd panicked.

Do they sleep in that mess behind the curtain?

Like…together?

It looks more like the kind of playpen you'd have rowdy sex in than somewhere to sleep. And while there aren't any rats out here, I wouldn't be surprised if there were fucking snakes in there.

Zachary tugs at the plastic ties around my wrists, and my eyes dart to him.

Was I staring? I've got to keep myself in check. I can't give them even a hint about what I'm thinking.

"What do you want from me?" I ask, hoping to distract him. Hoping to get some actual answers. They owe me that much after what had nearly happened up there. After what they'd nearly done.

Zachary holds out a hand. Cassius—who'd been busy rolling a weed cigarette on a nearby coffee table—looks up like they'd legit had some kind of telepathic conversation. He moves to the bookshelf separating their man cave from the library and opens a tin.

I almost don't hold my ground when the lamp's orange glow bounces off the switchblade he hands Zachary.

This is it.

This is why they brought me here.

They're a bunch of serial killers, aren't they? They hide out here and carve their way through whatever student they decide no one will miss.

Holy mother of God.

Is that what happened to all those students who Father Gabriel had told me disappeared in the woods?

I'm shivering. My skin is hot and cold at the same time. Zachary is staring at me, but I can't take my eyes off the switchblade. He drops his hand and flicks it open like a fucking professional.

My stomach drops straight into hell.

His hand darts out. I can already feel the blade sinking into my stomach. My eyes squeeze shut on instinct, and then flutter open a second later when there's no immediate pain.

He flicks the blade through my ties, releasing me.

My fingers tremble as I massage life back into my wrist.

Thank the Lord.

This will make it so much easier to escape.

He clicks his fingers as he points at the sofa furthest from the exit. "Sit."

"I'm not a dog."

He tilts his head. The orange light plays havoc with his eyes, turning them into surreal, gleaming orbs.

"Then don't make us tie you up like one," Cass says through a sneer.

I turn to frown at him.

In a flash, his fingers are around my throat. "Although you'd look real pretty in a collar."

Zachary lays a hand on Cass's arm, and he instantly releases me. Afraid he'll touch me again, I hurry over and take a seat where Zachary pointed.

"You didn't answer me," I say, making sure to use a neutral tone of voice.

Zachary drags a wooden chair to the space in front of my sofa. He seats himself at leisure, as if he's got all the time in the world.

"What makes you think you're in a position to ask questions?"

Reuben walks up to Zachary and holds out a short, thick tumbler. Amber liquid swirls around in it as it exchanges hands. Zachary throws it down his gullet and hands the glass back to Reuben.

I can't believe this is my psych teacher. Granted, I'd only had a handful of lessons with him, but I'd never thought he'd so much as touch a glass of alcohol, never mind sling it back like that.

Dad would have a nightcap before going to bed. I can still see him now, seated at his small desk in the corner of the dining room, a shot of brandy in one hand, the other slowly turning the page of his favorite bible. He would only ever have one glass.

Except when he returned from his missionary work with Father Gabriel. Then he'd drink like Zachary—tossing back shot after shot like he'd kept count of every nightcap he'd missed and was balancing the scales. Then he'd stumble off to bed and sleep for a day.

Mom said it was jet lag, and made her bed on the couch.

Then everything went back to normal.

Kind of, anyway.

"Answer him, honey tits," Cassius says. I flinch as he collapses onto the seat next to me. He has a glass too, but his still has alcohol in it.

"You want from me," I say.

Cassius sniggers.

"Information," I add hurriedly, willing my cheeks to cool down. "Else you'd have gotten rid of me already."

A bold claim. They could literally have brought me down here to finish what they started. But I know it's not that. Doing all sorts of dirty things to me in the shower hadn't been their intent when they'd trapped me inside there.

"We're just passing the time," Zachary says.

It can't be true, but there's nothing on his face to suggest otherwise.

How do they do it?

"I don't think so." I shake my head, and wrap my arms around my chest. It's not exactly warm down here, and I'm still only wearing my undies and a vest. The leather under my ass is deliciously cool on my tender rump, but it's freezing against the back of my thighs. I make a point of looking around their man cave. "You've got much better ways to spend your time."

Keep them talking. Learn something. And wait for your chance to run the hell out of here.

It's not the best plan, but it's *a* plan. A plan I can hold onto with dear life until something better comes along.

Cassius laughs and takes a sip of his drink. Then he produces a weed cigarette from his cupped palm and holds it out to me. I glance down at it, frown, and shake my head as I suppress a shiver.

"Here."

I look up. Reuben's holding out a big-bottomed wine glass with about an inch of alcohol inside. "This will warm you up."

He's definitely the member of this group I'm most uncertain about. While he gives off the kind of vibe that makes me want to climb over a wall to get away from him, he's the only one who hasn't hurt me or even threatened to yet.

Him and Apollo.

I take the glass from him and attempt a smile that probably comes out more like a grimace. "Thank you," I murmur as I take it from him.

He nods and disappears into the bedroom.

Cassius offers the cigarette to Zachary, who lights it and takes a deep drag before turning his attention back to me.

"How did you become friends with Father Gabriel?"

That's what they want to know? I shrug and bring the glass up to my nose. Whatever's in here is strong enough to make my eyes want to start watering. Maybe I should have taken that weed cigarette from Cassius instead. At least I wouldn't be hurting.

"He's my priest." I glance away, happen to spot a very dirty magazine, and hastily look back at Zachary. "Was, anyway."

"That's it?" Zachary takes another drag before passing the weed back to Cassius. "You said he was your best friend."

"He was, for a while." It's strange as fuck telling these near-strangers about my life. "Why are you so interested in him, anyway?"

Without warning, Cassius leans over and tweaks my nipple through my vest. I jerk to my feet in surprise.

He says, "We're the ones asking the questions," before I can get a word out.

Zachary clicks his fingers and points back at the sofa.

I want to throw my glass in his face. Not just the contents, the actual fucking glass.

"What changed?" Zachary asks in the same tone of voice he used a minute ago.

"He left our parish."

"Why?"

"He didn't say."

Zachary's jaw ticks, tensing like he's about to pounce on me. I crowd back into my seat, wishing I had something to protect myself with. I glance at Cassius, but he's staring down at the tip of the cigarette as if he's never been so fascinated by coiling smoke in his life. Zachary sits forward so quickly that I flinch. The contents of my glass swirl, almost spilling. His eyes go to the glass, and then back to me lightning fast.

"Drink it."

I hold it out. "I don't want—"

"Drink it!" His booming voice fills the room.

My hand shakes as I bring the glass to my lips and reluctantly pour everything in my mouth.

Cassius laughs when I start coughing around that fiery liquid as it sears its way down my throat. Then he snatches the glass from my hand and sets it down on the floor beside his arm of the sofa.

I wipe my chin with my fingers, and stare down at my thighs. My veins show up like tiny blue rivers under my skin.

Not sure how this is possible, but I keep forgetting I'm surrounded by crazy people.

That plan I had? A crock of shit.

I'm not getting out of here alive.

They're just toying with me.

The worst part is I'm starting to hope they'll at least take their time.

No one wants to die.

T*hump.*
   Thump.
Thump.

I try to ignore my pounding heart, but it fills every inch of my awareness.

Calm down.

Thump.

Thump.

Thump.

At best, I'd considered Trinity just another poor soul who'd somehow managed to get a ticket on the worst ride boarding schools in West Virginia offered. At worst, she was one of those crazy-eyed lackeys who follow Gabriel around like they couldn't wait for their cup of blue Kool Aid.

It had never crossed my mind that she knew him.

Not as the provost of Saint Amos, or the ex-bishop of Redmond.

That she knew *him*.

The horrific twisted demon possessing his corrupted body. A sinister entity we'd finally tracked down after years of searching.

She knew the *Guardian*.

Reuben brought her a blanket. He even tucked her in while I finished the blunt. Cassius immediately started rolling another joint. I had another shot of whiskey. That, with the weed, pushed my savage fury down to a level where I could communicate again.

"Why did you come to Saint Amos?" I ask.

Trinity glances up at me, eyes widening. "I didn't have anywhere else to—"

"Why?"

"My parents. They're—they were killed in a car accident."

"When?"

"About a month ago." Her eyes are bright, but no tears. Is she lying? Wouldn't make any sense if she was.

Rube takes the seat beside her. Framed between him and Cassius, her feet not touching the ground and her hair drying into wild curls, she looks like a little doll.

Cassius lights the blunt this time, takes a pull, and holds it out for her. She glances across at him and then down at the hands in her lap. The cuffs left bright red welts on her fair skin. I try not to look at them.

"This isn't me being polite," Cassius says.

"I don't want any."

"I could give a shit," he says, turning to her and leaning in. "Smoke it."

We know how this works. We've done it many times before.

It makes me sick to think of the things we've done to get to this point. Trinity should be on her knees thanking God we've already figured out torture isn't as effective as the more subtle means of interrogation.

The weed will make her chatty. The alcohol will make it more difficult for her to lie. Plus, it reduces her flight risk. Trinity takes the blunt from him and hesitantly takes a drag. Then another. She coughs, hard, and tries to give the blunt back. Cassius grabs her wrist and forces the filter against her mouth. "One more." When she complies, he murmurs, "Such a good little girl," into her ear.

She swoons when she sits back, and our eyes lock through a haze of dank smoke.

"Gabriel's been here for years," I tell her.

She nods, and then shrugs. "I didn't have anywhere—anyone else."

"What about foster care?"

"I almost had to." She nods a few times. "Because I couldn't get hold of him. But then he finally got back to me." She lifts limp hands and drops them again. "Brought me here."

"How long was he your priest for?" Cass asks.

She leans to the side, studying him for a moment, and then hurriedly straightens when this brings her into contact with Rube's shoulder. He's watching her as intently as I am. He looks like a fucking psychopath—hands on his thighs, back straight.

He tucks a stray corner of the blanket under her leg.

"Ten, twelve years?" She cringes away from Rube as if she wants to burrow into the stuffing. "I'm not sure. Maybe longer."

"When did you first join his church?"

"Gabriel's—?" She breaks off and frowns, shaking her head. "Maybe eight years ago?"

I glare at her. "You said you knew him for ten years."

"Or twelve," Cassius supplies unhelpfully.

She shrugs. "He was friends with my dad for a while before

we moved to Redmond. That's when we joined his church." She slumps a little. "What is this all about? Why do you—?"

"Pour her another drink."

I wasn't even looking at him, but it's Rube who stands to fulfill my order. Trinity waves a limp hand.

"I really don't want—"

My eyes slide to Cass. "Tell Apollo to search her room. Make sure she's not hiding anything."

Cassius is on his feet in a second, loping to the exit like a panther that's finally spotted something to pounce on.

"Hey!" Trinity sits forward, her tits bouncing behind that pathetic film of a vest. "You can't do that!"

"We can do whatever the fuck we want," I growl.

She stands in a rush and charges after Cassius, and I'm less than a beat behind her. I grab her shoulder, hauling her back. Her vest rips as she twists to knock away my hand. Then she's fumbling with herself, trying to cover her bare naked breasts.

"Ooh, can it wait?" Cassius croons from the exit, his voice moving closer. "Her roommate might spot him—?

"That fucking queer?" I snap. "Jasper won't say a word. Trust me." My eyes never leave Trinity's, not even to look at her tits.

"Fuck," Cassius mutters, and then there's just the swish of the drape.

Trinity tries to draw the torn halves of her vest back over her chest, and flinches when I tell her to stop.

"How close are you with Gabriel?" I ask, stepping up to her. She moves back until her shoulders collide with a bookshelf.

"We're…friends."

"He ever fuck you?"

Her eyes go wide, and color instantly suffuses her cheeks. "What? No! He's…he's my fucking priest."

"Was," comes Reuben's voice. He thrusts out her glass, now half-filled with whiskey. "Now he's nothing."

"He's still my friend," she says, ignoring the booze. "He's never done anything to—"

"So he's never touched you?" I close the distance, snatching the glass from Rube's hand on the way.

"No!" Her eyes sparkle with anger.

I grab her chin, force it down, and tip the glass against her lips. "Drink."

She turns her head, spilling whiskey down her throat and bared breasts.

"I'll lick that off later."

At this, her body goes rigid. That same light sparkles, but this time it's not anger. It's not even fear.

Weed's really good at several things. It makes you chatty. Happy. Hungry. Horny.

This little thing in front of me must be so fucking confused right now with her body throwing so many conflicting signals her way. I want to believe her.

"I saw you with him," Rube says as I steer the glass back to her mouth and wrench open her jaw. "You're more than friends."

She doesn't get a chance to reply, because I'm pouring whiskey into her mouth. This time, she catches it. Swallows it. When she coughs, some it sprays on my face.

I tear off what's left of her vest and use it to wipe my face.

She starts crying.

Those big fat crocodile tears insult me.

I jerk her forward and bring the flat of my hand down on her ass with a solid thump. Her tears cut off in an instant. She sniffs, still trying to cover her tits, but no longer being pathetic about all this.

"We never—I'm not—" She chokes on whatever she'd been going to say and hangs her head.

"But you want to," I say.

Her eyes dart up, still brimming, but she blinks away the tears before they can fall. "No."

"Of course you would." I slide a hand to the small of her back and draw her with me as I move to the couch. She comes with me, unresisting but unsteady. "Handsome fuck like that." My stomach churns, but I swallow down the bile that comes up and keep going. "You must have imagined what it would feel like?"

"No," she lies, her voice barely a whisper.

I sink onto the couch and draw her down with me. She takes her original seat, and glances warily at Reuben when he comes to sit beside her. He holds out her glass, and she lets out a forlorn little sigh.

Finally, the fight is over.

That last shred of resistance drains from her body. Her eyes dull to sullen gold as she drops the arms she'd been using to cover her chest. We don't look. Right now we couldn't be bothered with her tits. It's her mind we've been trying to lay bare.

She was right. We didn't bring her down here to fuck her. We came down here to interrogate her.

Torture never works.

Victims will say anything to get the pain to stop.

Weed and alcohol, though?

The combination leaves them helplessly compliant.

She lets Rube feed her the last inch of whiskey. When she shudders as the booze hits her throat, her convulsion reaches me through the seat cushion. Before I can stop myself, my hand's around her throat. I push her back against the couch, and she lets me. There's not even a sliver of fear in her eyes—just hopeless abandon.

Do your worst, Zachary.

Snuff out my life like the others. Why not? What else could I possibly tell you that you don't already know?

But then it hits me.

It's not what I need from *her*.

It's what *she* needs from *us*.

If she honestly thinks this friend of hers is the pure, innocent priest from her past, then we need to set her straight. It's a pity, having to break something so pretty…but at least the four of us will be there to pick up the pieces.

"How do you want him to fuck you?" My voice comes from far away as I start to disassociate from the moment, from what I'm about to do.

Her pulse quickens under my thumb.

"Like in the drawing," she says. Her lips curl up into a faint smile. "The one Cass—Cass's—ius drew."

"You can call him Cass," I murmur, leaning close, applying a little more pressure on her throat. She squirms a little, her eyelids flickering. But she's been numbed to everything—panic included.

It's better this way.

I know from experience.

Rube's hand enters my view. He fixes the rosary around Trinity's neck, positioning the crucifix just-so between her heaving breasts. Then he trails his fingertips down the center of her body.

Her stomach convulses at his touch, fluttering like a butterfly's wing.

She giggles.

I flinch at that innocent, happy sound as it wrenches me back into the here and now.

My hand tightens. I shove her back hard enough to dislodge Rube's hand and to recapture her attention.

"Did he ever touch you?" I ask again.

"*No,*" she gasps. "*Never.*"

"Good." I sit back, releasing her throat and flexing my fingers.

Rube lays a hand on her stomach, and it nearly covers her belly. "You should be thankful," he says.

Trinity rests her head back, slowly bringing a hand to her throat. She strokes the faint marks I left behind as her eyes move to Reuben. "Why?"

Her voice is thick now, her tongue sluggish as it forms the word. I guess she wasn't lying when she said she doesn't drink. She's minutes—perhaps even seconds—from passing out.

"He would have defiled you," Rube tells her mournfully. "Just like the others."

TRINITY

"...*T*ake *it to...drinks it all.*"

I open my eyes to orange-tinted darkness. It feels like someone's standing on my head. They may, possibly, be the same culprit who rubbed grit in my eyes. I push onto my hands and glance around.

I'm in their bedroom. This should alarm me. Terrify me, in fact, but I can barely think straight through the sullen *thud-thud-thud* of my head.

Orange light slices a line across the myriad blankets and pillows scattered about. I blink at the silhouette a few times before I recognize it.

Apollo comes over to me, stepping in and around the mattresses like he's walking a minefield. He crouches beside me and holds out a steaming cup. "Coffee," he explains. "Cream, two sugars. That right, pretty thing?"

I can't even.

I nod at him and accept the cup. Thankfully, my ass barely hurts anymore, so I can sit up in a cross-legged seat as soon as he disappears out of the room.

After a quick check to make sure there are in fact no snakes around, I drag a blanket over my shoulders. It's absolutely freezing in this place, and no surprise—it's not as if the library has heat.

The guys talk in hushed voices for a few seconds, and then there's utter quiet.

I spill coffee into my lap when Zachary calls out my name.

"Trinity? Join us."

I consider ignoring him.

Then I remember his warning. I don't need another hiding, thank you very fucking much. Juggling the coffee cup, I somehow manage to drag a blanket over my shoulders without spilling a drop. Then I make my way to the other side of the man cave.

They're all seated, Reuben and Cassius on the same couch I was on, Zachary still in his chair—although it's been pushed back closer to the bookshelf now—and Apollo on a badly worn armchair on the other side.

They all look up when I enter, making me freeze.

"Are you hungry?" Reuben asks.

Am I—?

I glare at him.

Do these freaks think they hit some kind of reset button when I went to sleep? What the hell is wrong with them? They've assaulted me, kidnapped me, *and* interrogated me, all in a matter of hours.

What. The. Actual. Fuck?

I still don't even know why. It has something to do with Gabriel, but Lord knows what.

Something inside me snaps. I storm forward, coffee sloshing dangerously close to the rim of my cup. "No, you sick fuck, I'm not hungry!"

I expect one of them to say something, maybe to try and calm me, but they keep staring like they paid good money for this show.

Setting down my coffee on the closest bookshelf, I keep the blanket closed with one hand and use the other to point at Zachary.

"You think you can just go around doing whatever the fuck you want? Well you're wrong! You can't."

Zachary settles back in his seat and crosses his arms over his chest. Is that a smile ghosting his lips?

"Someone's going to notice I'm gone. You realize that, right?" I scan the other faces one at a time. Apollo with his mop of unruly hair. Reuben with his ten-yard stare. Cassius who—

He's fucking *leering* at me. "Who's gonna notice you're gone, my little slut?"

"Stop calling me that!" I charge forward, emboldened by their apparent lack of giving a shit. I make to punch him on the shoulder, but nothing close to that happens.

Instead, he's on his feet pulling some kind of ninja move that has me draped over the back of the couch and him bending over me.

No one stops him.

Cass's hand slides under the blanket, grabbing at my breast. Reuben's rosary falls out and dangles from my neck.

"How did you sleep?" Reuben asks, as serene as fuck. Contorted like this, I can barely breathe. The fact that Cass keeps groping me isn't helping.

"Okay!" I shriek. "Please."

"Let her go," Zachary, by contrast, sounds exhausted.

"God damn it, Zac!" Cass pushes away from me, but not before he squeezes my ass with both hands. "Stop giving me fucking blue balls."

"You're doing it to yourself," Zachary replies. "Now sit. Both of you."

"Yeah, right over here," Cass says, showing me his teeth as he drags me around the couch.

I end up on his lap, despite my protests. He seems to remember Zachary could get me to stop fighting with a slap on my butt, so it takes three of them before I sink onto his lap and don't bolt straight up again.

It's not exactly the most comfortable seat. Does he *always* have a hard-on?

"Where are your things?" Zachary asks.

I glower at him for a second, and then remember how futile it is to resist, protest, or fight back. "What things?"

"Trinkets and keepsakes and shit like that," Apollo fills in. I glance up at him, but his eyes are on the camera in his lap. He seems intent on either fixing it, or taking it apart piece by piece.

"I don't have things like that."

"You didn't bring any with you?" Zachary asks.

"No. I don't *have* things like that." I cross my arms, mimicking him, and shrug. "What, is everyone supposed to have a whole bunch of junk for no reason?"

"Things of sentimental value?" Zachary says. "Most, yes."

"All I found was this," Apollo says, leaning over and picking up something off the floor beside his armchair.

I would have stood if Cass hadn't slipped an arm around my waist and clucked at me like I was seconds away from receiving another smack. So I toss my hair and try and make it seem like I don't give a fuck that they've taken the only thing I brought with me that wasn't clothing or shoes or underwear.

"It's a bible," I say stiffly. "In case you were wondering."

"An old translation," Zachary says, stretching to take it from Apollo. He flips it open, and I tense…waiting for the photo to fall out.

After how they'd grilled me about Gabriel, what would they say if they saw the photo of him and my father? It might spark the kind of reaction that ends in violence.

But nothing falls out. Either they've already found it, or I jammed it so hard between the pages that they'd have to open it to the exact place to take it out.

I can only hope they've been too busy to check.

Zachary hefts the thick volume in his hand. "I prefer these. The newer translations are too… polished."

"They've taken out all the good shit," Cass agrees. "All that fire and brimstone."

"Strange how many things are open to interpretation," Zachary muses, as if to himself.

"Mis-interpretation," Apollo says. The camera comes apart in his hands, and he stares at the assortment of pieces now littering his lap.

"Not everything."

I turn to Reuben, and swallow when I see him staring at me. When he reaches for me, I instinctively close my eyes. They pop open when his fingertips brush my breastbone. He lifts the crucifix dangling around my neck and rubs his thumb along the wood. It releases a sweet, heady scent that makes me squirm on Cass's lap.

Which, in turn, makes his erection even harder.

"Enough!" I snap. I yank the crucifix from Reuben's finger and turn to glare at Zachary. "Tell me what the hell I'm doing here."

Now my head's thumping like a bass drum. I press the heel of my hand against my temple, wincing, but I don't break eye contact with Zachary.

He sits forward, resting his elbows on his knees and lacing his fingers together. "You, Trinity Malone, are going to help us take down a sex trafficker."

I laugh, because what the hell else am I supposed to do? "Me? How?"

Zachary goes on as if I hadn't spoken. "They called him 'Guardian'." His jaw ticks. "You know him as Gabriel."

There's a beat of silence where even my heart stops beating.

Zachary gives me a grim smile. "Sorry. *Father* Gabriel."

My coffee's gone cold in my hands. They gave it back to me a few minutes after they'd started telling me their story.

Apollo begins.

"My parents got shot when I was six. Mugging gone wrong kind of thing. I'd been an altar boy for like a month before that happened. Somehow, I ended up at an orphanage in Redmond instead of foster care.

"Not that I minded. I thought it was kinda cool. Had a lot of friends to play with. I was there for like a year before it happened."

He pauses, and starts collecting all the bits and pieces in his lap and putting them on the floor, arranging them around his bare feet.

"One of my teachers told me I'd done so well in class that he was taking me out for pizza." Apollo lets out a sardonic laugh. "Fucking idiot I was, I believed him. That's how easy it is to get a kid into your car. Fucking pizza, man."

He sniffs, and drags his hair out of his face. It flops back again, but he doesn't seem to notice. Zachary lights something. I first think it's weed, but then cigarette smoke billows into the air between us. They start passing it between them, each taking a drag or two before passing it on.

"We drove for hours. What it felt like, anyway. I started getting cranky. He slammed my head into the dashboard so hard I passed out." Apollo scratches at the scar on his forehead like he can still feel that pain through the years.

And here I'd thought it was an old sports injury or something.

"When I came to, I was tied up in a basement." He starts arranging the various mechanics of his broken camera around his feet in a halo.

It feels like someone's pouring cold water down my spine. He takes a deep breath, and glances up at Zachary.

Zachary nods at him.

Apollo looks at me.

That icy water freezes, and my entire body goes stiff.

"I had two Ghosts. They'd come every Saturday and Sunday, alternating like." He sticks out his fingers and twists them back and forth. "Never saw each other, but they timed their shit so well, they had to have wiped each other's cum off their dicks more than once."

My mouth fills with saliva. For a moment, I'm convinced I'm going to puke. Cass takes my wrist and urges my cup to my mouth.

I take a sip. "Ghosts?" The word slips out before I can stop it.

Apollo's eyes dart up. His foot starts tapping. "Yeah, Ghosts." He points at Reuben. "He came up with it."

"It's what we called the men who visited us," Reuben says. I glance at him, but he's still staring at Apollo. "We never knew who they were, or how long they'd stay. They weren't supposed to speak to us."

"But some of them couldn't shut up," Cass says.

I look at him over my shoulder. His blue eyes could have bored a hole through my head. "I got there a few months before Apollo arrived," he says.

"Where? In the basement?" I glance over at Apollo. "The same one?" Apollo seems to have forgotten I exist. He's busy with his camera again.

"Yup," Cass says. "Now snuggle up, honey tits. It's my turn."

ZAC

I need another blunt, but I light a cigarette instead. We know we don't smoke less when we share, but it's been a habit of ours for years already. Back when we first met, it took a lot for us to share anything, even our names.

Trust becomes addictive. Dangerously so.

Cass drags Trinity against his chest, arranging her like a sleepy kid—her head on his chest, her legs folded to one side. She lets him, but I think that's because she's in mild shock.

Or just really hungover.

"I was a handsome little shit, even back then," Cass starts. He toys with Trinity's hair, winding her curls around his finger as he talks.

It's surreal, listening to them. Stories spooling out like snagged threads from their tangled hearts. I've only ever heard snippets. Partial retellings whenever we'd discovered a new clue that led us deeper into the web of lies the Guardian had spun to keep his enterprise hidden from prying eyes.

"They must have been watching me for a few months already. I recognized the car they used when they finally snatched me.

Broad daylight, the fucks. But they knew what they were doing. Where I'd be, at what time. That's I'd be alone."

Cass smooths a hand down Trinity's head, and it looks as if she burrows against him. "I lived in a small-ass town back then. The kind where your kid could take the bus from elementary school and you knew he'd get home safe and sound."

She shifts, tilting back her head, and shakes her head.

"But I didn't, did I?" Cass says as he tweaks the tip of her nose. "It was one block from the bus stop to my house. A five-minute walk. That day, I never made it home."

Trinity widens her eyes. Cass paints the outline of her lips with a fingertip.

"I didn't make a fuss. The minute I saw the car, I already knew what was happening. I don't know how, but I just knew. I tried to run, but they had one of their guys on the sidewalk ahead, and he just grabbed me and shoved me into the car."

Cass stops touching her. He looks away, his head dropping and his eyes clouding with dark shadows.

"They injected me with something. Knocked me clean out." His head snaps up, and he points straight at me as he grins. "I woke up next to James. You remember him?"

I don't say anything. Cass has the floor now.

He turns to Apollo, then Reuben. "You guys remember James? Fucker with the crazy eyes?"

I almost laugh.

I'm sure if we had to ask Trinity, she'd say we *all* have crazy eyes.

"Anyway." Cass waves a hand. "I had a shit ton of Ghosts. Didn't even bother keeping track." He bestows her with his radiant grin. "Guess I've always been a good lay." He winks at her, making her shy away from him.

None of us bat an eye when Cass glosses over his abuse. It's how he deals with his shit, just like we all have our little quirks and idiosyncrasies.

To each their own.

Trinity peeks at me without lifting her head. "How many boys did they...?"

"We're not sure." I shrug as I take a pull of my cigarette before handing it across to Cass. "Things were erratic. I assume on purpose."

"And the others? What happened to them?"

I push the inside of my lip against my teeth and chew on the skin. "That's not the question you should be asking right now."

Her brow furrows. She pushes up and away from Cass, making him groan theatrically. Then she carefully slides off his lap, as if worried he'll claw her back.

He won't.

As much as he likes to make out he was the furthest thing from a victim, he *did* suffer. He was the prettiest of the bunch. We all were—that's why they kept us for so long. Other boys would come and go, but our Ghosts seemed incapable of letting us go.

Fuck that, who am I kidding?

Of *disposing* of us.

Cass won't be feeling frisky for a while. He'll start acting out like he always does when he's forced to recall his past. But he drew the short straw, just like Apollo.

We try to be fair to each other. As fair as we can be without turning into complete and utter pussies.

"The Guardian. He wasn't a Ghost?" Trinity asks.

The cigarette, having traveled all the way around our circle, comes back to me. I tug at it before killing it in the ashtray.

"Not to our knowl—"

"Of course he is!" Apollo cuts in. Trinity jumps at the sound of his voice and turns wide eyes to him. "Just because he never touched us, doesn't mean he didn't…" He throws up his hands.

I wait him out to make sure he's finished. "To our knowledge, no."

"So how do you know he's involved?" Trinity's voice rises an octave higher.

"Because everything always leads back to him," I tell her. Then I sigh and sit back, running my hands through my hair. "The four of us—" I swing out a hand to encompass my brothers "—we lived together in that basement for years. Boys would come and go, but we'd stay behind. Some of the Ghosts started talking to us. We started piecing things together."

"Then we escaped," Reuben says.

I point at him. "Then we escaped." I exhale into the silence as Trinity leans forward with an expectant frown.

"And then?"

Traces of smoke from deep in my lungs wreathe my words. "And then everything went to shit."

TRINITY

I t's inappropriate to laugh after what Zachary said, but I have a hysterical need to giggle.

Then it went to shit?

"I don't understand," I say, carefully swallowing down any mirth that dares to bubble up. "I mean, did they catch the Ghosts? How does that lead to Gabriel? None of this makes sense!"

Zachary shakes his head. "None of the men who molested us were ever arrested by the FBI or the police. Not. One."

I hug myself, and burrow deeper into my blanket. "Why? Didn't you have enough evidence?"

"Oh, we had evidence—" Apollo begins, but he cuts off when Zachary throws a hard stare his way. I guess his turn to talk is over.

I haven't heard Zachary's story yet, or Reuben's, but I'm already at the point where I want to tell them they're making this up.

And even if they're not, there's no way Gabriel could be involved in something like this.

No *fucking* way.

"Two arrests were made," Zachary says calmly.

"That's it?"

He nods once. "There was a trial. The suspects were sentenced to death."

My eyes go wide. The blanket creaks in my hand as I tighten my grip. "As in...the death penalty?"

Another nod. "They'll be executed next month." There's that tick again. He clenches his jaw as if he's suddenly aware of it, and swallows. "The investigation was closed a long, long time ago. According to the feds, they found everyone involved."

"Tell her about Gabriel," Reuben says. "She has to know."

Zachary holds up a hand. Licks his lips. I've never seen him this unsure of himself, and it makes panic flutter deep in my belly.

Earlier, they seemed convinced Gabriel was, *what?* Some kind of kingpin? The guy responsible for all their pain and suffering.

Zachary opens his mouth, but he can't seem to produce words.

For some reason, that terrifies me.

A hand lands on my shoulder. Reuben turns me to face him. It's unreal, seeing such deep pain on such a young, vital face. He could have been the poster boy for a high school football team.

"I'd always beg my Ghost to tell me why he was doing what he was doing." Reuben slaps his palm into his chest. Apollo flinches. "Why *me?*"

My mouth goes dry and goosebumps race over my flesh.

His black eyes trap me like tar.

"He said I should ask the Guardian. That he could explain it."

I'm hanging on every fucking word, but Reuben's struggling

with this as much as Zachary was. His wide chest rises and falls as his breathing becomes slow and deep.

"I told him—" Reuben burrows a hand into the top of my blanket. I don't fight him—by now I know what he's looking for. He takes hold of my crucifix and rubs the wood. It seems to calm him, because a level of tension leaves his face. "I told him I didn't know who the Guardian was. That I only saw him. So he told me—"

His voice grows thick. Rosewood hits my nose how hard he's rubbing that crucifix.

"Rube," Cass whispers from behind me. "Bro, you don't have to—"

"The Guardian said we were the cure." Black eyes pin me. "That the Ghosts had a sickness. We kept their symptoms—those urges—at bay, so they could do their jobs." His breath hitches. "So they could preach the Word of God without being plagued by their desires."

My mouth falls open. Without thought, I lift my hands and wrap my fingers around Reuben's fist. My chest closes rendering speech impossible, but there's nothing I could have said anyway.

Nothing.

"When they were done—" He pauses to swallow. "When their visit was over, they would meet with the Guardian and confess their sins."

Reuben's hand trembles inside my fingers.

"And he would bless them, and make them pure again."

He lets go of the crucifix, taking back his hand and slowly putting them face down on his thighs.

"Until their urges came back, of course," Zachary says.

My heart fucking bleeds for these boys. I rub a palm over my collarbones, willing it to go inside and easy the ache they caused.

"Then the whole sick cycle would start all over again." Cass leans close, sliding his hands over my shoulders. "All with the help of your BFF."

I shake my head, and it frees a tear from my lashes. "No," I whisper. "Please. I'm sorry about this. What happened to you. It's...it's fucking wrong and disgusting." I haul in a breath and stand on shaky legs, turning to look at them. "But Father Gabriel didn't have anything to do with this. I *know* him. He's a *good* man. He's always been there for us."

Four stony faces watch me.

"Please. Believe me. It's not him. He's not your Guardian."

Fabric rustles behind me. I whirl around as Zachary gets to his feet.

"We thought you'd say that." He cocks his head and slowly scans me up and down. "And you're right. We don't have any proof. Not a—"

Reuben sucks in a breath, but keeps quiet when Zachary holds up a hand.

What had he been going to say? Surely if they *did* have proof, they'd tell me?

"Not all miracles are divine, Trinity." Zachary slides a hand around the back of my neck and draws me closer. I move on wooden legs, too entranced to even think of resisting. "But you? I swear on my life you were sent by God Himself."

"What?" Is all I can manage.

"That proof? *You're* going to find it for us." His hand tightens cruelly, wrenching a gasp from me. "You're going to bring it to us. And together we, us five..." He comes close enough to kiss me, for his commanding eyes to fill my world.

"We'll make him give us the names of our Ghosts."

I don't want to know what comes next. Cold dread is already spreading through my limbs, going for my heart.

"And then we'll catch them." His brushes a curl from my

face. "And we'll inflict on them every wound, every pain, every bit of shame they inflicted on us."

My heart bangs against my ribs. "Okay."

"And then we'll kill them." His eyes don't change in the slightest. "Okay."

Behind me, three voices chant one word in unison.

Amen.

I should be horrified at myself.

But I'm not.

I'll prove to these damaged, tortured souls that Father Gabriel is the kind and loving man I know him to be.

And if, somehow, everything they say turns out to be true?

Well, then, I guess I've signed a deal with the devil.

A-fucking-men.

To Be Continued...

Trinity and the Brotherhood's story continues in Their Will be Done...grab the next book in the series, or binge read the rest of collection today (PLUS a bonus, exclusive novella) by downloading the entire trilogy boxset.

https://authorloganfox.com/sosa-boxset

Can I send you my secret dark romance novella that's never been published...?

Join my VIP newsletter and you'll receive your own exclusive copy of My Darling, and I'll keep you up to date with my new releases and promos!

https://authorloganfox.com/my-darling-signup

MORE BY LOGAN FOX

For more books by this author, reading order, playlists, trigger warnings, socials, and more…please visit:

https://authorloganfox.com